P9-CDE-717

THE
HOME
PLACE

THE
HOME
PLACE

by

WRIGHT MORRIS

CHARLES SCRIBNER'S SONS, NEW YORK
CHARLES SCRIBNER'S SONS LTD. LONDON

1948

For

CLARENCE MILLARD FINFROCK

ACKNOWLEDGMENTS

To Henry Allen Moe and the John Simon Guggen-heim Memorial Foundation, I owe the support, material and otherwise, which made *The Inhabitants* and *The Home Place* possible.

I should like to believe that the books them-selves—pioneer enterprises in the field of publishing —are a witness to the traditions and integrity of Charles Scribner's Sons.

THE
HOME
PLACE

To be at all critically, or as we have been fond of calling it, analytically, minded—over and beyond an inherent love of the general many-colored picture of things—is to be subject to the superstition that objects and places, coherently grouped, disposed for human use and addressed to it, must have a sense of their own, a mystic meaning proper to themselves to give out: to give out, that is, to the participant at once so interested and so detached as to be moved to a report of the matter.

HENRY JAMES
THE AMERICAN SCENE

THE HOME PLACE

WHAT'S the old man doing?" I said, and I looked down the trail, beyond the ragged box elder, where the old man stood in the door of the barn, fooling with an inner tube. In town I used to take the old man's hand and lead him across the tracks where horses and men, little girls, and sometimes little boys were killed. Why was that? They didn't stop, look and listen. We did.

"Is he planting melons?" Clara said.

"No, he isn't planting melons," I said. Clara put her hand over her glass eye, drew down the lid.

"If he isn't planting melons it would be nothing useful," she said.

"He's fixing his inner tube," said the boy.

"Thanks son," I said, and put my hand on his head. After the girl I wanted a boy so I could stand with my hand on his head, or his shoulder. But you can't. Try it sometime. I took my hand off his head and put it on the cool handle of the dipper, pressed on the handle, and skimmed off three drowned flies. I showed them to the boy and said, "Sprinkle them with salt and they'll be as good as new ones."

"How's that?" said Clara.

"I was just telling the boy to feed flies like that to the chickens." I opened the screen, and tossed the water into the yard. Four or five seedy leghorns ran through the shadows, scratched for them. "You see that, son?" I said.

"I told him to bring fresh water," she said, "but I don't think he's got around to it. He's eighty-one. He don't get around too much."

"You're not so young yourself," I said.

"I'm a farmer's wife," she said, and pulled a green stocking cap low on her head. My Aunt Clara is a raw-boned woman, a little over six feet tall, flat as a lath, and with the stalking gait of a whooping crane. In the early morning she wears a bright green stocking cap. She's been doing that for at least thirty years —against the night air, as she calls it—the tassel dangling over the

1

ear that once troubled her. It gives her a certain rakish look. "I'm a farmer's wife," she repeated, and picked up a small tin bucket, with a blue Karo label, and started across the yard. She seemed to wade through the soft, pitted chicken mounds. "There's not a square inch of this yard," she said, without turning to look at me, "them chickens haven't scratched from one place to another one." She walked behind the hedge fencing the drive, where I could see the bright glint of her cap, like a whip tassel, jogging along toward the barn.

"What you looking at, son?" I said.

He was out in the yard, his head between his knees. He picked up something, smelled it, put it down again.

"What you got there?" I said.

"Nothing—" he said, and stood up.

"Suppose we take these pails," I said, "and get Grandma some nice fresh water?" I took two pails from the table on the porch, gave the boy the short one, with the blue and white stripes. I took the milk pail with the wooden handle, the tall straight sides. "When I was your age," I said, "I used to fetch fresh water every morning," using the word *fetch* advisedly. I nodded my head toward the pump, where the old man was standing, fooling with his tube, before I noticed how close to the house it seemed. The last time I fetched water that pump was a block away.

"What's this?" the boy said, and kicked at a bump he saw in the yard. He kicked it loose, and it rolled across the yard into the weeds.

"That's a croquet ball," I said, and looked around the yard for the wickets. When I was a boy I tripped over those wickets all the time.

"Cro-kay?" said the boy, "what's cro-kay?" He was standing with the ball, scratching off the layers of dirt. Under the dirt was a faded orange band, he sniffed at it.

"It smells like the subway," he said.

There you have it. There you have it in a nutshell. Two thousand miles from New York a city boy turns up something in a farm yard, it smells damp and earthy, like a storm cave, so

he calls it the subway smell.

"You think it smells like the subway?" I said.

"It's smelly," he said.

"Put it down," I said, "before your sister has to sniff at it." He put it down, wiped his fingers on his clean city pants. Peggy is worse than the boy in the sense that she can't see, feel, or smell anything, without comparing it with something else. God knows what she would think that ball smelled like.

"What's cro-kay?" said the boy.

"Let's get that water," I said, then seeing the old man I added, "suppose you ask your Grandpa. He's the man to answer questions like that." We picked up our pails and walked down the trail toward the old man.

"Thinks I—" the old man said, "tube as heavy as that'll last forever. Well, says he, would if it was rubber, but it ain't rubber. What is it, says I? Airsuds, says he. What's that, says I? That's what it is if it ain't rubber, says he."

"Where's the handle to the pump?" I said.

"Airsuds, says he. That's what it is if it ain't rubber." The old man hung the tube around his neck and put the boy's bucket on the pump nozzle. He pulled on a piece of taped wire that went into the pump house. A motor started. "Hole in it as big as my head," he said, and squeezed his finger into the nail tear.

"This new rubber is not so good," I said.

"It ain't rubber," said the old man. "It's airsuds." He liked that word. He spit and watched the water spill into the pail.

"What's cro-kay?" said the boy.

The old man took the small pail off the nozzle, hung on the milk pail.

"This boy pullin' my leg?" he said, but without looking at him. He gazed across the yard at the hay rick, the break in the trees.

"You've got to remember," I said, "this is the first time he's been out in the country. In the city you don't have yards like this. You don't play croquet."

"I didn't play it much," the old man said, "but I knew what it was."

"You had it right here in the yard," I said. "The boy's never had a yard. If he had a yard like this he would play croquet."

"Seems to me somebody might've told him what it was."

"He never asked before," I said. "There's two or three hundred thousand boys in the city who never heard of croquet. They don't know what it is. What's more," I said, "they don't want to know." Was he listening? He had turned his back to me to spit.

"Viola's kids were born and raised in Lone Tree," he said, "but they know what croquet is."

"Lone Tree—" I said, my voice a little high, "is not New York. There is no grass in New York, no yards, no trees, no lawn swings—and for thousands of kids not very much sky. They live in cages," I said, "it's like a big zoo of kids. A cage with windows and bars."

"Seems to me a man with any sense, or any kids, would live some place else."

I managed to keep control of myself by picking up the pail. I put it down again and said—"You may not know it, but there's several million people, Americans—" I added, "without a decent place to live. They live in trailers, tents, and four or five people to one room." I stopped. My voice came back at me from across the yard.

"Two empty houses—" the old man said, his voice flat, and wheeled to point at them. He pointed east, then directly across the road. My hands were shaking so bad I didn't want to risk spilling the water. I put my left hand on the pump nozzle. It was cool. "One across the road," he said, "be empty in a week or two."

I wet my lips and said, "I thought Ed lived across the road."

"Ed's sick—" he said.

"He's sick?"

"Be dead in a week or two." The old man spit, stepped on the quid like it was a bug. "Didn't see him for ten or twelve days, so Clara thought I'd better look over. He was in bed. Lyin' there. Well, says I, ain't it about time you was gettin' up? Well, says he, it's in my legs. What, says I? I can't move, says he." The old man felt in his pocket for his pipe, tapped the bowl on his palm. He took out a ten-penny nail and scratched the ashes off the top. "Couldn't twitch his toes. Been lyin' there eight or nine days."

"God almighty," I said.

"First thing I did was give him somethin' to get a little movement. Set him on the potty. Held him like a kid. Guess he hadn't been to the outbilly for ten or twelve days."

"Where's he at now?"

"Bed in town with a lady to watch him. Day and night. Well, says I, ain't you a little old for this kind of tinkerin'? Says he, I ain't too old to enjoy it."

I put my hand out toward the boy, but he ducked. "You want to help your Grandma look for eggs?" I said.

"I want to know what cro-kay is," he said.

"Ask your daddy later," I said, "run along now and look for some eggs."

"How'd he know where to look for eggs?"

"Well, I've told him a thing or two," I said. "After all, his daddy was born on a farm."

The old man looked at me. He twanged his nose between his thumb and forefinger—"I thought you was born in Lone Tree?"

"Lone Tree is a small town," I said, "and I was born on the edge of Lone Tree. We had a horse and some chickens. We had a cow—for a while," I said.

"I didn't think you was born on a farm," the old man said. He picked up the smaller pail and started for the house.

As my boy was eyeing me, I said, "I could walk right from here and put my hands on some eggs. I used to do that all the time. All summer," I said.

"I'd think about it first," the old man said, "as them old hens are gettin' pretty touchy. They catch you foolin' with them eggs an' they'll cackle half the night." Alongside the corn planter he came to a halt, put down the pail. He took the inner tube from his neck and looped it around the seat post of the planter. "Come to think of it," he said, "used to wonder why them chickens was so fretful in the summer, and in the winter was just as nice an' quiet as you please." He gazed across the yard, toward the shade elm and the house, where the croquet court used to be. "My, them Plymouth Rocks was sharp—let it get a little dark an' they come in along the drive. Them fool leghorns get tangled in them wickets, every time."

"You know where an egg is?" the boy said.

"There's your sister," I said, and pointed at Peggy standing in the door of the barn. She's a good deal like her mother, so I said— "What have you been into?"

"Nothing—" she said.

I put the pail down and walked toward her across the yard. She was holding her new apron like she had made a muss in it, but instead of running she waited for me. I came up and looked at the white egg in her lap.

"That belongs to the chickie," I said, in her mother's best manner. "It's the chickie's egg. It isn't our egg. We'll put it back."

"The chickie gave it to me," she said.

"All right," I said, "go find Grandma and show her what the chickie did." She started off. "Take your brother along," I said.

"I've got my hands full *now*," she said, and sighed like her mother.

"What's cro-kay?" said the boy.

"There's your mother at the screen," I said. "She's been help-ing Grandma. Canning. Let's both take your mother a nice cool drink." I went back to the pump for my pail, but when I looked around the boy was gone. The barn door was swinging, and two swallows were noisy on the wires.

"See those birds?" I called to my wife. "They're barn swal-lows. They live in the barn."

"Not a bad idea," my wife said.

That could be taken several ways, but not right at the moment.

"How's my little dove?" I said, and smilingly walked toward her. But I seemed to have forgotten how to carry those milk pails. I put it down and looked at the water on my white buck shoes.

"Parboiled—" she said, in answer to my question, then— "If you're going to play at being Old McDonald you can first come in here and change your clothes."

"When I was a boy—" I said, biding my time, "there was a fine clipped lawn right where I'm standing. I used to mow it. Play croquet every afternoon."

"Where are my babies?" she said.

"They went off to find some eggs," I said, and left the pail where it was till I had changed my shoes.

My wife opened the screen, then let it slam and followed me into the kitchen. Clara's beets were cooking on the cob range. There were newspapers spread on the table and over the lid of the water bin, with lapping red beet rings from the dripping mason jars.

"Boy!" I said, "Pickled beets!" and took a deep breath.

"Suppose you stand right there and inhale it," my wife said.

"Now look here—" I said.

"I didn't come out here," she said, "to be parboiled in another woman's kitchen."

"I don't know as she asked you to," I said.

"What do you expect me to do?" she said. "Sit in the front room in the rocker while she's out here parboiling?"

"That's a good word," I said, "so long as you don't overdo it. You keep telling me you were born on a farm, so I just took it for granted you could live one day where the old lady's lived all of her life."

"I *can* carry a bucket of water," she said.

"If you think you can control yourself," I said, "it might interest you to know that I've located a house. Right here in the neighborhood." That calmed her.

"We can't furnish a house right now," she said.

"This house is all furnished, all ready," I said. She looked at me. "You don't *have* to pickle beets," I said, "there are other things you can pickle, and I suppose you've noticed how your babies like the farm." She had. "But a good deal depends on your being able to control yourself. If they thought that one afternoon in the kitchen was more than you could stand—"

"Suppose you walk over there and lean over that stove," she said.

"You seem to forget," I said, "that I was born and raised out here."

"I've often tried to," she said, "but I can't."

"If that's the way you feel," I said, "suppose you call the kids and tell them we're leaving." I went to the screen, cleared

my throat, and called, "Oh Peggy!"

"Are you absolutely crazy?" my wife said.

"Don't worry," I said. "She won't come."

"The least you might do," she said, "is try to understand how I'm feeling. I wasn't born out here." She looked at the stove. "And I don't like pickled beets."

"You've never tasted a real pickled beet," I said, and walked into the front room, where it was cooler.

"If it's like her *real* fried egg," said my wife—"Why it was vulcanized. I couldn't cut it."

"That will be enough of *that*," I said.

"What makes me so sick," my wife said, "is that you can't take it as well as I can. I'm at least polite. I don't yell at them like a fishwife."

"I was not yelling at him," I said.

"Well, you raised your voice," she said.

"He always makes me raise my voice," I said, "but I was not yelling at him. He's not very well informed, and you can't tell him anything."

"You ought to try and tell *her* something," she said.

"I'll tell you what it is I can't stand," she said. "It's *all right* for you to share their lives. That's fine. But they don't give a dam about yours."

I walked through the dining room to the front door that Aunt Clara had always kept locked. It was still locked, as they had never put a porch at the front of the house. If she left it unlocked, the old man, or some stranger, might have killed himself. The old man was forgetful, and sometimes gave the door a try.

My wife came in and said, "I'm just all nerves from this housing situation. It's all I can do to just try to be nice—"

"I'm a little touchy, too," I said, "but I am trying to do something about it. For one thing," I said, "I have just driven your babies two thousand miles."

"You're very sweet."

"These people think we're crazy," I said "—if they think about us at all, but it doesn't keep them from sharing their own house. They'll share what they got, including their vulcanized eggs."

"I didn't mean that—" she said, "but I couldn't cut it—either."

"The old man thinks I'm a total loss, but you notice how he offered me what he smokes?"

"What *is* it?" said my wife.

"Airsuds—" I said. "That's what it is if it isn't tobacco." I walked into the small room at the side, where my wife slept with Peggy, and looked at my face in the bureau mirror.

"You're sunburned—" she said, and looked at me in the mirror. "Does it have to be so dark in here?"

"She's trying to keep it cool," I said, "for people like yourself. She used to have a lot of trees, nice big shade trees, but they died in the drouth."

We stood there and I could hear the chickens cackling.

"What about this house?" she said.

"If you can just keep your mouth shut," I said, "I think I've got my hands on a house." My wife took out some pins, put them in her mouth, and let down her hair. She ran her fingers through the braid and said—

"What house?"

"If I remember correctly," I said, "Ed's house has a john and running water. He put it in for his mother. I don't think he married anyone."

"Ed who?" she said.

"Uncle Ed—" I said. "On Clara's side."

"What's the matter with him?"

"He's sick," I said. Then I cleared my throat and said, "The old man says he's a goner. In a week or two."

"I didn't come two thousand miles," my wife said, "to do what they're doing in New York."

"No—?" I said.

"Well, not exactly," she said. "I'm not going to budge until he's really dead."

"That's being really thoughtful," I said. She didn't pick that up, so I said, "It's a small-type house, one floor and an attic," and I raised the blind a foot or so and looked at the road. There were still a few trees, mulberry and catalpa, but I could see the front of Uncle Ed's house. I remembered him as the owner of an Edi-

son Gramophone. I liked the horn and the felt-lined case of black cylinders. "Pretty nice for the kids," I said, "they could spend a noisy day over here, then come home and spend a quiet night with us."

My wife came to the window and said, "So it's come to this."

"You can be dam thankful it has," I said.

"I wonder what it's like inside?"

"There's just one floor," I said. "That window opens on the attic. The thing to remember is the running water and the inside john."

"That's important," she said, "seeing as how you can't carry a pail of water."

I ignored that and said, "You can't judge the place on how it looks now. This was some farm," I said, "thirty years ago. The old man had a five acre orchard with the finest apples in the state; he's got a trunk full of the ribbons he won at the fair." That reminded me of something and I said, "I wish you could have seen the old lady. She won all of the jelly and quilting prizes they had around here."

"What happened?" she said.

"You wear out," I said. "Out here is where people and things wear out. You keep winding it up till one day the ticker stops."

"Can't they get any help?"

"You can't get farm help any more," I said. "Men will do anything rather than work on a farm."

"Women, too," she said.

"Sure," I said, "women too."

"It makes you wonder, doesn't it?"

"The old man's an awful dam fool," I said. "You can't tell him a thing—but there's something about him."

"There's always something about an old fool," my wife said.

I left her there and walked through the house to the back porch. Aunt Clara and Peggy were coming in from the barn; Clara was tipped away from the bucket I had left near the pump, and Peggy was carrying the Karo can, full of white eggs. I walked back to the folding doors and said, "Well, here she comes."

"Do you have to shout?"

"If she left you here with her beets, all I've got to say is you better be here."

"Hmmm—" she said.

"If you can just control yourself," I said, "I'll have you a nice little place in the country. But you leave it to me. Just try and control yourself." I took a quick look at the stove, to see if anything was burning, then I went upstairs to change my clothes.

The stairs are right behind the range, in something like a steep chute—one of the reasons you can't live up there in the summer time. I could feel the heat right through the plaster wall. As a boy I had the room at the head of the stairs, where the ceiling slopes down over the bed, but on hot summer nights I slept on the floor. The windows were low, and there was sometimes a breeze down there. As my own boy is about that age— eight next October—I had an odd feeling when I got to the top of the stairs. Put it this way—for a moment I wondered who I was. Since we left New York, a week ago, I'd been trying to tell my boy, whenever he'd listen, what it was like to live on a farm. You can't do it. You can't tell a city kid anything. But I had talked a good deal to myself, and lay awake thinking about it, which might account for the feeling I had. I was Spud Muncy, sometimes known as "the little fart."

Whoever I was, I was facing Viola's room with its flower- cluttered wallpaper, and the handcolored photo of her skinny brother, Ivy. Ivy had been seven that summer, but he was not a little fart, in any respect, so he had been able to wear my clothes. That's my fauntleroy he's wearing on the wall. He was also wearing my high button shoes, and my pink Omaha garters, which showed all right, but not in the photograph. I sat in the buggy and thumbed my nose at him. I was wearing his cast-off rompers, with the drop-seat and the dark brown stains, and while thumbing my nose I was smoking licorice cigarettes. A good deal of my spit was there on the buckboard, beside the old man's.

I was facing Viola's room, and Ivy, but when I turned on the stairs the door to the old man's room—their room, that is—stood open. All of the upstairs rooms are dark, as the windows are low, floor level, and the blinds are usually drawn against the heat. All the light was on the floor—I used to lie there and read. Mid-

summer nights I would lie near the window and read the Monkey Ward catalogue, the descriptions of watches, long after the old folks had gone to bed. As my father always talked a good deal, in bed, I used to wonder why these people, who went to bed so early, never said a word. Their shoes would drop on the floor, that was all. I would hear the old man puff at the lamp—sometimes he had to whooosh at it—then the dry rattle as he settled back on the cornshuck mattress. Some nights, for quite a little while, he would yawn and burp. Thirty years ago he often complained of what he called a weight in his stomach—a stone at the pit of it, he said. Whenever he complained at supper, he burped at night. My father always said no human could live on a diet of potatoes and pork gravy, but the old man is alive, and my father is dead, now, ten years. I lay awake the night before, thinking of that.

I suppose after fifty years of marriage there may be things to keep you awake, but not much for you to lie in bed and talk about. If you pile out of bed around a quarter past five, single plow a foot deep with a team of deaf mares, at a quarter past eight the odds are you'll be ready for sleep. Sometimes I'd hear the old man sit up, and use the potty, or hear Clara tell him, in her high private voice, that it was storming and he had better put the windows down. That was one thing he could do. Would do, that is.

I went to the window and raised the blind so I could look at the seedy elm, the leaning cob house, and along the untrimmed hedge toward the barn. The chickens had made a spongy pit of the yard. That accounted for a good deal of the wormneck, and the stumbling gait I had seen among the hens, as you can't let chickens mess around in their own dirt. But you couldn't tell the old lady that. After a little more than twenty years, four of them at the state Aggie college, Ivy managed to tell the old man a little bit about hybrid corn. Not much, but a little bit. But he could never tell him to move his machines in out of the rain. Or to vaccinate his cows, or his pigs, against the cholera. No, you couldn't tell him anything. Years ago, when I was in school, I sent the old man a pound can of tobacco, a fine blend I couldn't afford to smoke myself. I also sent him a French brier, a small

bottle of pipe sweetener, and an English-made cleaning tool. He sent everything but the tool back to me. "I thank you for the tool," he said, "which I got right here in my pocket, but Granger's the only cut I get any satisfaction from." No, you couldn't tell them, show them, or give them anything. They were like the single plow below my window—when the old man had a piece of plowing to do he hitched up his team of mares, and that was what he used. A foot deep and a yard wide, stopping at the end of the furrow to sit on the crossbar and spit on the white grubs at his feet.

"It's men like him," Ivy had said, "who made this goddam dust bowl."

True enough—but it was men like him who were still around when the dust blew away. As my wife said, there's always something about an old fool.

"Oh, Dearie—!" my wife called.

"Coming—" I said, and sat down on the edge of the bed to change my shoes.

Clara was making a place near the range for her basket of cobs. Peggy stood there, with her bucket of eggs, and before I looked at her she said— "The chickies gave them to me, didn't they, Grandma?"

"I suppose they did," Clara said, and picked up a handful of cobs.

"Don't just stand there gaping," my wife said, who was standing there gaping, "do something." I took the lid holder and raised the stove lid, Clara dropped in her cobs. I raised the lid on the cob bin, to look inside, but it was empty.

"I don't use it any more," Clara said. "With my wrist like it is I can't lift it." She took the poker from a hook on the wall, pushed the cobs back in the range.

"The chickies gave them to me, not to Bobby," Peggy said.

"They're still the chickies' eggs," I said, "until Grandma sells them to the grocer. Then they belong to whoever wants to buy his fresh country eggs."

Clara put down the poker, "Who in heaven's name you talking to?"

"I was talking to Peggy," I said. That didn't explain very much so I said, "If she's going to understand the world she lives in, she's got to learn about buying and selling. She's got to learn why it is we pay for things."

"Is there anyone that don't know that?" Clara said.

"The world is full of people," my wife said, "who don't understand the simplest things."

"Children are logical—" I said, "if you just take the time to explain things to them."

"Just what are you explaining?" Clara said.

I looked at my wife. "I was explaining—" I said, thinking, "why it was first of all the chickie's egg. Why it was the chickie's egg before it was her egg, for instance."

"Money is the medium of exchange," said my wife, "but how many people really know it?"

"I thought everyone did?" said Clara. "I thought that was the trouble."

"Seven out of ten people," said my wife, "think it's something else. They think it's something in itself. The one thing you can say about Russia—" My Aunt Clara had been stooping for cobs. She let them drop, stiffened to her full height. That left her free to look right over my head at my wife, who turned as if someone had walked up at her back.

"Peggy Muncy—" she said, "you in your right mind?"

"Aunt Clara—" I said, and picked up two jars of red beets, "where shall I put them?"

"Right back where you found them," she said, and let the lid snap up on her glass eye. When she was upset it was hard to tell which eye it was. They both had a high sparkle, and a hard, clear shine. I put the jars back on the same red rings, fit them, you might say, then I stepped back and wiped the sweat off my face.

"Peg—" I said, "you mind finding me a handkerchief?" Without waiting to see if she would I stepped out on the porch, drank two dippers of water, then splashed one on my face. I wiped my face on the towel and watched the PILLSBURY stamp come up, slowly darkening, like a print in the developer.

I stood there, trying to cool off, but it's either my wife or

one of her babies.

"I want to buy some eggs," Peggy said. "To buy some fresh country eggs I need some money." The way we keep our children from asking for money is to keep them supplied with it. I took out two nickels, gave them to her.

"Ask your Grandma what eggs are worth now," I said. "Ask her what fresh eggs bring a dozen."

"Tell him to ask the chickens," Clara said, "they're the chickens' eggs."

"Your Grandma is a very smart woman," I said, and wagged my head to show I really thought so.

"She's not a plain darn fool," Clara said, and went back to her beets.

"Suppose we buy our eggs later," I said, and winked at Peggy, which I do on such occasions, but she didn't wink back, which was what she usually did. She didn't press the point, however, about the eggs. "There's your brother and your Grandpa," I said, "out there near the barn. I wonder what they're doing?" She put the pail of eggs down and came out on the porch. "Why don't you go see what they're up to?" I said. From what I could see the old man was showing the boy a spotted kitten. "Why, that looks like a little baby kitten," I said. Peggy pushed on the screen, very slowly, then she walked out near the ragged box elder. She stood there, in the shade, looking at them. She was just like her mother. So damned independent you wanted to scream.

"Is it such a proposition to raise a child?" Clara said. She turned with the mason jar she was holding to place it, upside down, on the paper. She waited for it to ooze. It didn't ooze. She tried another one.

"The world is such a mess, Aunt Clara," I said, "you can't blame people if they want to try something, if they want to raise their kids a different way. They want the world to be different. You can't blame them," I said.

"How do you want it?" she said. "Your powder wet or dry?" She tipped another jar of beets and said, "The world ain't such a mess it can't be a worse one."

"Some people doubt that," I said.

"Then they should know better than to have children. You want to hold this for me?" she said. "It's my wrist." I held the jar, and she screwed up the lid.

"It's pretty hot weather for canning," I said.

"I've seen it a good deal hotter," she said, "and I've seen it cooler. I can tell hot and cold." Maybe I'd forgotten she could be like that. I wiped my hands with the towel and tried to think how to turn that one. I couldn't.

"You want to help me here," she said, "or you busy keepin' your hands clean?" I put the towel on the rack and took a good grip on the jar.

"What's this I hear about Uncle Ed?" I said.

"I don't know," she said, "unless you heard he was dying."

"That's what I heard." She didn't go on, so I said, "Ed's lived a long life, guess we can't live forever."

"Nobody has," she said. That was all.

"Ed never married, did he?"

"No, he never married."

"I suppose you've been wondering," I said, "just what to do about the place." She nodded. "If I know Uncle Harry," I said, "he wouldn't want a bunch of strangers right across the road. You have to be particular. You wouldn't want just anybody living over there."

"No, not just anybody."

"A man living over there would cross the road, naturally, if he had to borrow something. That can be nuisance."

"Indeed it can."

"It would be nice," I said, "to keep it in the family."

"That's what I had in mind when I wrote to Ivy."

"Ivy—?" I said, "but Ivy's got a farm."

"If Ivy was across the road he could farm Harry's eighty. It ain't been farmed, now, since the war."

My wife had come to the door. She stood there, twisting the handkerchief I had asked her to get for me. Before I could shut her up she said, "I don't suppose it matters if people with children, and no place to go, needed a home?"

"Peg—" I said, "it's none of our business what Clara does with Ed's farm. There's other people who need a place to live as well as ourselves."

"It may be none of *your* business," she said. "But I'm their mother. It's mine. And I'm not going to pussyfoot around about it."

"All right—" I said, "I'm washing my hands." I washed them. But it wasn't all right. Aunt Clara looked at me, drawing the blue veined lid over her glass eye. "Aunt Clara," I said, "I just happened to mention that Harry said Ed's house would be empty. I suppose you know we're looking for a house?"

"I declare," she said, "but a house isn't a farm. Do you farm?"

I'd forgotten about that.

"He could learn," Peg said. "All he does is talk about the country. He says the country is the only place in the world for kids."

"That still doesn't make me a farmer," I said.

"You mean to say you can't learn?"

"A farmer is a farmer," I said. "You grow it. You don't learn it."

"Peggy Muncy—" Clara said, "you mean you want to live on a farm?"

"I want to live," my wife said, "and I don't care where it is!"

"Less than an hour ago," I said, "you were pretty dam particular," then I shut up, and watched my wife tear up my handkerchief. She tore it, carefully, in five or six strips, squeezed them into a wad, then stepped forward and threw the wad in the pot of beets. I might as well admit that's why I married her. She didn't throw them on the floor, where an ordinary female has her tantrum, but she threw them into the beets, the pickled beets, where they belonged. Then she turned on her heel, and before I could tell her the front door was locked, or head her off, she had walked slam-bang right into it.

Over ten or twelve years you learn whether to interrupt something like that, or to go about what is sometimes described as your own business. I stared at the beet jars, resting upside down on the yellow back copies of *Capper's Weekly*, and wondered what it was, in cases like this, Clara had learned. Over fifty years she had learned something. I have an irritating habit of getting upset over nothing to speak of, but being calm as hell when a

real crisis comes along. I was calm enough, standing there, watching my Aunt Clara hold her eye as if my wife had leaned over, socked her one. Her teeth were chumping, which is a habit she picked up from Mother Cropper, and didn't, in some instances, mean anything. In her left hand she still held the poker, and as an example of how calm I was, I took it out of her hand, casually fished out the handkerchief. Hot pickled beet juice makes a pretty good dye. I let the strips drip for a moment, then I dropped them into the cobs, wiped off the poker, and hung it on the wall.

"When does Ivy plan to move in?" I said.

I looked right straight at Clara's good eye, which is blurred and a little faded—not so good, really, as the strain has worn it out. This is the kind of nerve, the kind of calm, the mean in heart have. You get it after ten or twelve years in the city—it's the kind of spunk that makes good alley rats, Golden Gloves champions, and successful used-car salesman. It doesn't take much nerve to sell used cars, but I always like to bring in used-car salesmen, all of them, when I have reference to something pretty low. With this kind of nerve I stared at Aunt Clara, and after a moment it occurred to me that I—we, that is—had her buffaloed. She had never seen the like of us before. She had never seen a woman, with two children, throw a well rehearsed hanky-tantrum while her husband looked on, admiringly. Simple folk don't know how to deal with vulgarity. They're puzzled by it, as real vulgarity is pretty refined. You don't come by it naturally. Maybe you can tell me why it is that simple folk are seldom indelicate, while it's something of a trial for sophisticated people not to be. You can't put in an evening, with really smart people, without a good deal of truck with what is nothing more nor less than vulgarity. If you get to be good at this sort of thing you can bring it out in the country, like the shell game, and fool the yokels with it. After all, I tell you, these crude looking people are delicate. They're soft when it comes to real vulgarity. I'd say the whole myth of the city-slicker is built around that softness, and the fear they have of this complicated kind of indecency. They take a man at his face value, as they figure it's his own face, a fairly private affair, and the only one he has. They don't roll the eyelids back to peer inside of it. They don't leer at you with the

candid camera eye. They lead what you call private lives, which is not so much what you know about them, as what you know is none of your dam business. That's a good deal. A smart city man would make use of it.

Now I'm not a good city man for nothing, so I said, "You've no idea what it's like to live in a big city, Clara—to try and raise a pair of kids in a place like New York."

"I don't know as I'd want to know," she said. I looked at her, remembering what my wife had said. *You can share their lives, all right, but they don't give a dam about yours.*

"It might give you some idea," I said, "why Peg just threw a tantrum. Why it is we're both, in some ways, just a bundle of nerves." She waited. "I don't know whether it interests you," I went on, "but if you had some idea of how we've been living, for the last ten years, we wouldn't strike you as being so strange."

"Well, you're that," she said.

"I'm a Muncy," I said, "as much as Uncle Harry. If he'd been wearing my shoes for the last thirty years he would strike you as silly as I do."

"I doubt that," she said. She tipped her head forward to think about it, and stared at the floor. "Take a good deal more than thirty years," she said.

"What I'm trying to suggest," I said, "is that I am a Muncy, my kids are Muncys, but that living in the city is not living on the farm. It does different things to you. But you're still a Muncy underneath."

"You think you have to tell me that?" she said.

"I don't know," I said, "what I have to tell you. I'm trying to get my bearings. I'm trying to feel at home out here." I looked out the window, at the yard, and said, "Something happened out here, in four or five summers, that thirty years of hell and high water, and twenty years of the city, has not changed in me. That's what I want for my kids. They're Muncys—" I said, "that's what they deserve."

"They're nice enough youngsters," she said.

I turned back and said, "You think Ivy would rent us a room?"

"My land, what would you do with a room?"

"We could put the kids in it."

"Why, you know very well they're all right here."

"Maybe I could put Peg in it," I said.

Clara straightened and said, "I just wrote to them—they're not yet in the house."

"If you've written to him," I said, "that's that."

"Why, if I know Ivy," she said, "he wouldn't think of putting you out. If you asked him you could have it. He's like that."

"When you've got two kids, Clara—" I said, "it makes you pretty selfish. Ivy have any kids?"

"He's hopeful—" she said.

"Maybe Ivy has some idea," I said, "what it's like right now in New York. What it's like to have a pair of kids in a place like that." I walked to the side window and said, "Ed has a nice little place—too bad Ivy hasn't any kids to enjoy it."

"You'd need a double bed, for one thing—" said Clara, "but maybe you could have Viola's. It's up in her room. She has one of her own."

Another thing hadn't occurred to me. It hadn't really occurred to me that no matter what I said, or how I said it, it would be taken for the truth. In the world right at this time there probably weren't too many people, grown-up people, who would ever know what that was like. You can't cheat. That's an odd feeling.

"Who'd Ivy marry?" I said.

"Genevieve."

"A local girl?"

She looked at me. "I forget," she said, "how long you been away." I pulled out a chair from the table and sat on it. "Warner," she said, "Genevieve Warner."

"Warner?"

"From Battle Creek."

I waited. Then I said, "She's a good girl for Ivy?"

"Why, she's a Warner," Clara said.

That's that. Vital statistics: Genevieve Warner, Female, Battle Creek. But what about Genevieve? Nothing. Not a word. *She's a Warner* engraved at the base of the monument. When I ask my wife she says— 'Fay? Oh, the horsey type, nasal A, Bryn

Mawrish. Not too complicated.' Not too complicated—is that Genevieve?

"She's a farm girl?" I said.

"My land," said Clara, "she's a Warner. Didn't you and Ivy play with the Warners?" I nodded my head. "Well, she's the stem-wind one of them."

To sit on a straight-backed chair I have to lean forward, on my knees, and look at my hands or something on the floor. On the floor was a piece of worn linoleum. The center of the pattern had been worn off, and Clara had daubed on one of her own. Brown and green dabs of the brush. Uneven rows. I looked through the door at the dining room, the dark-wood chairs spaced on the wall, the cabinet in the corner, the harvest-hand table, the single frosted bulb on the fly-cluttered cord. Everything in its place, its own place, with a frame of space around it. Nothing arranged. No minority groups, that is. No refined caste system for the furniture.

"Ivy was set to marry her," she said, "then the war came along and they had to put it off. Six more years. That makes twelve years in all." Twelve years is how long I've been married. Ivy is a year younger than I am, so the way I would calculate would be that he had been waiting for eleven years. "That's a good deal of time, when you're young," she said.

"That's too long."

"Indeed it is, but with a war on what can a man do?" I looked at the floor again and decided that the pattern was part of the floor. It was not decoration. That was why she had daubed one on again.

"Is Genevieve the one we called Potty?"

Clara shook her head. "I wouldn't know."

"She was pretty tubby back then," I said, and saw Potty Warner, pretty well pimpled, holding a grasshopper while he spit at me.

"During the war she went to business school for a year. She was with Mr. Crile, in Battle Creek."

If you wait you can piece it together a little bit. Farm girl, about thirty-two, with a taste for J. C. Penney pumps, McCall's shirtwaist blouses, rimless glasses, and the Sears & Roebuck Book

Club. But no feminine hygiene, lipstick, or cutrate jars of Mum.

"How long they been married?"

"Four months Thursday," she said, and looked at the calendar on the wall behind the Kalamazoo Brilliant. I could see a penciled circle around April 9th.

"I suppose they would like a family?"

"Well, I should think," Clara said.

"That's fine," I said. "Now that's fine."

"Harry wouldn't say a word," she said, "but the one thing on his mind right now is a boy. Viola has a boy but he's a Stokes. He's not a Muncy."

"I've got a boy," I said. "He's a Muncy."

"I know—"

"My name is Muncy," I said, "and I have a male child named Will Muncy," which was true enough, but no particular point in my saying so. What kind of Muncy had never heard of croquet?

"It's been a long time since we seen you—" Clara said, and took her hands from beneath her apron, put them on the chair arms, let herself down in her rocker. She rocked, her right eye covered, and looked at me. I did not look at her with my camera eye. I looked at the floor and the hole she had worn in the patch of linoleum, and the hole beneath the patch, by rocking and dragging her heel. Every time she rocked forward, the right heel dragged back. Where she walked without her shoes—in the morning and evening—the linoleum had a high shine from her cotton stockings and narrow bare feet. "Viola's girls are all Muncys," she said, "in everything but the name."

I heard my wife's powder puff slapping her nose. Before I could get up, or head her off, she came into the room and said, "For one thing, little girls are usually brighter. They've made enough tests now to prove it." That's the way she is, you bat her down and she's right back up.

"I don't know as they're smarter," Clara said, "but they're different. Viola herself was a good deal different."

"All this talk about boys—" my wife said, "you would think little girls were not even human. What's wrong with little girls carrying the name?"

"I suppose nothing much," Clara said, "it just happens they don't."

"Besides—" said my wife, "what is there in a name? I'd just as soon have the name Stokes as the name Muncy."

"Seems to me," Clara said, "you're neither a Stokes then or a Muncy. If you was either the name would mean something."

For a good many years my wife, Peggy, has never been shut off. A man named Plinski once shut her off—a dog meat butcher, on 48th street—and in the course of time I gave him a box of Bering cigars. But that was long ago, and my wife was new to the world. Nothing like that had happened since then so we were both caught off our guard—the only proof I need, if it ever comes up, to make my point. I let her feel what it was like, for ten seconds or so, then I gave her a straight look and said— "I was telling Clara here about Mother Chudder—wasn't she the one who went out to Ohio?"

"Hmmmmm—" said my wife, and stood there looking at her nails. That's precisely what she did the night a big ham named Witherspoon exchanged a dance with me—a Witherspoon for a Muncy? There you have it in a nutshell. I could have hit her with the poker but I said—

"Peg's people are all over the east, Clara. I guess Grandma Chudder is up in her eighties now."

"Grandma is eighty-*six*," said my wife. I like the old lady a good deal better than most of her family, but I wasn't overcome by the fact that she was still alive. She was one of these Grannies who had maintained a good second rate mind in first class condition, which led people to think she was a good deal brighter than she was.

"How old is Mother Cropper now, Clara?" I said.

"Mother's ninety-seven Friday," Clara said.

Well, that settled *that*.

"If she keeps on," I said, "she'll be in the same class with Grandpa Osborn," which was true enough, in its way, as the old man was dead. Getting back to the subject, I said, "Peg's folks have a place near New York, but with two kids you need a house of your own."

"It's the kitchen—" Clara said, "you don't like another

woman messin' it." Once you really shut a woman off you can do quite a bit before they recover. But don't overdo it. Leave well enough alone.

"We were in one room for two years," I said, "so a place like Ed's would be like a mansion."

"Maybe you'd like to walk across and look at it?" Clara said.

I looked at my wife. "I know I'd like it very much," she said.

"It's Ivy—" I said. "If I thought that Ivy—"

"He wouldn't think of it with you needin' a place." She pushed up from the rocker and took a key from a nail near the stove. "We keep it locked. Ed always had a fear of city prowlers."

I took the key and walked out on the back porch.

"You're welcome to stay here—" Clara said, "till we know how it is with Ed. If it's a turn for the good he can put up with me or Viola."

I stepped out in the yard just as a car turned in from the road. The hedge along the drive is six feet high, but I could see a white plume of steam, like a locomotive whistle, all the way to the barn. At the end of the drive it swung into the yard, rattled across the harrow, bounced in the hen pits, then died with a great hiss of steam. Through the mist I could see Ivy, a piece of burlap in his hand, trying to unscrew the cap on the radiator.

"Why, there's Ivy now," Clara said, just as the cap blew off, and a jet of rusty water settled on the windshield, blotting out Genevieve.

I hadn't seen Ivy Muncy for twenty-eight years. I said something to this effect as we stood there, shaking hands, and his level gaze roamed about over my head. Ivy's more of a Cropper than a Muncy, which is Clara's side of the family, and he has her rangy build and lath-flat frame. I never think very much about accents until I meet somebody I've known years ago, and find they sound a little queer. Ivy's voice was pitched high, for a big man, and though he opened his mouth when he spoke, the sounds seemed to come from some vibration behind his nose. Not through his nose—a noise with which I'm familiar—but behind it, as if his cheek bones were a sounding board. He seemed to feel that himself, as he twanged his nose, like a zither, with a thumb

stroke quite a bit like the old man. He was dressed for town, as Clara said, in a blue serge suit, striped cotton shirt, and a pink straw with an enameled artificial look. The straw was new, with that Valspar shine they bake onto cheap hats, and a creaking sound when he honed the brim, tipped it back on his head. In spite of all that, I would have called him a good looking man. I took a glance at my wife, as I favor her in these matters, but she was standing with Clara, looking at Genevieve.

Potty Warner was still tubby enough. A little woman with a cracked mouth, mousy hair, and denim-blue eyes, she wore the mail order version of the Town and Country bride. She was holding a red plastic bag, which didn't help her color any, and wearing a small organ-monkey hat, with a tight chin strap. Her weight had shifted a floor, since I knew her, lending an idle look to her arms, but rooting her legs firmly in the ground. My wife was telling her how much she liked her hat.

"Jenny—" Ivy said, taking her arm, "you remember Clyde, don't you?"

"We been talkin' about him all the way over," Jenny said.

"I don't mean that," Ivy said. "I mean you remember him to look at?"

"He's good to look at," she said, "if that's what you mean."

Maybe I'd forgotten Potty Warner could be like that. My wife turned to look at me, and I said, "Well, you're not so bad to look at yourself, Jenny—" which is an example of what flattery will do to a man.

"We've heard so much about you," Jenny said.

"Indeed we have," said Ivy.

"You've heard about me?" I said, feigning surprise. I was really surprised, but I've got in the habit, over the years, of feigning it.

"Jenny's got it home now," Ivy said.

"It—?" said my wife.

"Your picture," he said. "She found it in some magazine or other and cut it out."

"The open throat one?" my wife said. Jenny nodded. "They all like that one," my wife said. "*All* of them."

"Well, it does look like him," Jenny said.

Now I'm not well known at all, but it's too much trouble to

explain to people, honest people, that any dam fool might write a book. It so happens I'm not a dam fool, but that's even harder to explain, so I end up, on the whole, keeping my mouth shut.

"Was this in the *Times*?" my wife said. "There was a nice little piece in the *Times*."

"In the *World Herald*," Jenny said, "it was called 'Creative Native.'"

When I heard that title I looked over Jenny's head, at the barn. The old man had stopped to peer in the door. I could hear the kids somewhere in the back, the boy's feet running across the hayloft, and the giggle Peggy has when she has pulled a fast one on him. Very likely she had trapped him in the loft.

"Are you teasing your brother?" my wife said, just as the boy began to holler. Then he stopped hollering and said, "I'll tell Grandpa!" Not his father, nor his mother. He said "I'll tell Grandpa."

The old man chuckled, scratched the back of his head. Sometime during the morning he had shed his coat and exchanged his nautical hat for a moth-eaten felt, with a rakish tilt to the brim. It curled quite a bit like one I used to wear. I had forgotten that the old man used to favor hats. All his other clothes he could hang on one post of the bed, with a bar to spare, but he kept five or six different hats on Clara's stove. I remember him facing the glass in the cupboard to set one on.

"Now who's that little rascal?" the old man said, and looked at the kitten Peggy brought him. "That's Mike," he said, "don't think he likes huggin' like that too much."

"I'd say my best creative work," I said, as the boy grabbed the old man's hand, "is the two small volumes you see there in the door of the barn."

"Your work?" my wife said, "that's my work!" which is not so bad if you haven't heard it too many times before. As it happens I have—every time I've said it—but it sounded fairly good there in the yard. We all turned to look at the kids, Peggy with the spotted kitten, and the old man's hand flat on the boy's head. Now as I've said, the boy doesn't care for that sort of thing. But he stood there like a post, as if the old man was leaning on him, and my wife slipped her hand in the pocket of my

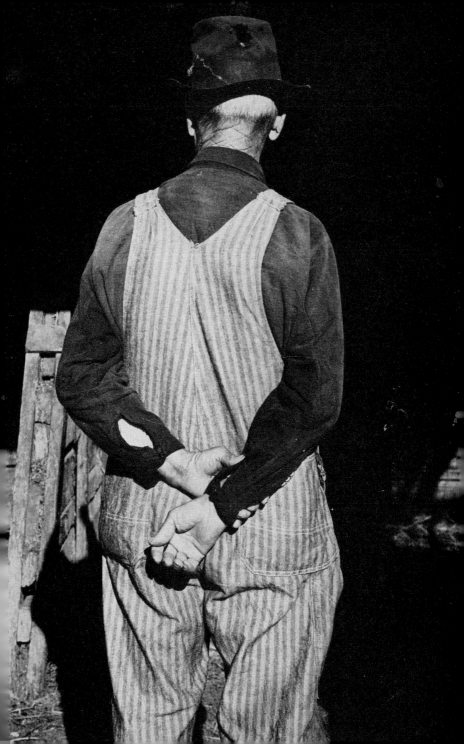

coat. That's where she keeps her compact, and my own hand happened to be there.

"My, what a pretty kitty," my wife said.

"The pussy gave her to us," Peggy said.

"That's a him," said the old man. "Mike's a boy."

"The pussy gave *him* to us," Peggy repeated, which was odd, in its own way, as I can't remember her having said *us*, like that, before. "She gave him to us," she said, and then waited till the old man's hand had wiped his mouth, and dragged across his seat, before she reached for it.

We followed the old man and the kids toward the house. Although his hands were empty there was a curve to his shoulders, and a weight to his walk, as if he were carrying two full pails. Aunt Clara went ahead to open the door, as if she alone knew how to unhook it, then she let it close, with a bang, just as we pulled up.

"Ivy—" she said, "before I forget, I told Peg here that she and Clyde could have Ed's house, if they wanted it. They don't have a thing, and I said you'd want them to have it first."

"Now Clara—" I said.

"You got a place, Ivy," she said, "and though it's not just what you want, it's a place, anyhow, and a roof over your head. Peg here don't have a thing."

"This is Ed's place?" said Ivy.

"Ed's place," Clara said.

Ivy fished out a toothpick from the pocket of his shirt. Jenny had been facing Clara and my wife, but she turned and looked at Ivy, who was munching the toothpick, staring over her head. He took the toothpick out and said, "We was more or less plannin' on it, but if Clyde here needs a house, why then it's his." He took off his straw and wiped his hand around the imitation leather band. "Isn't that what you say, Jenny?" he said.

"Why yes—" she said.

In a bad situation I'm calm enough—in others I'm not so calm, and have the habit of plucking my ear, or energetically picking my nose. My wife pulled my hand down and said— "I can't tell you how much we really need it. We've both been nearly crazy with the kids."

Peg's got into the habit, recently, of using the word *frightful* in practically every connection with the word *house*. I was proud of her for not using it. It would have been another one of those subway smells in the yard.

"We want to thank you very much," I said, setting a tone for Peg to follow.

"We really do," Peg said. I was proud of her.

"What about Ed?" the old man said, putting his hand on my boy's head again, "seems to me he's the one to thank." He looked gruff, to make clear it was quite a joke. The old man has a dry, scaly humor and as fine a dead pan as Buster Keaton. I laughed, and he said, "Well Ed, says I, have I got to live another five years to get a pretty girl to sit and talk to me? Well Harry, says he, if I was the girl I'd make it ten. Maybe by that time you'd learn how to behave yourself." He took his hand from the boy's head, and as we walked into the kitchen he hung his hat on the dipper handle, left it there.

"You have to leave that hat on the dipper?" Clara said.

"You can't stop a chicken from scratchin'," he said. "You ought to know that," then he tipped forward to spit on the cobs.

When I'm in good humor I'm pretty good company. With that housing business off my mind I was willing to listen to the ladies, or the old man, discuss almost anything. The weather, the crops, or myself, for instance. We sat in the living room, where the shades were up, with the ladies on the thin-lipped chairs, facing the light, and the old man in his rocker hitched around to where he could look through the screen. Ivy sat on what had been Viola's piano stool. The piano was gone, with Viola I suppose, but I could see where it had been in the clean square on the flowered wallpaper. The flowers there had a fresh, artificial look. Over this square, in an oval frame, was the picture of three wild horses, their manes flowing against a dramatic stormy sky. That picture once hung over my bed as Ivy had been very fond of horses, and I shared his room in the summertime. I wondered what he thought of horses now. He was holding my boy between his legs, showing him some jiu-jitsu business, something he had learned in the army, I suppose. It was hard for me to picture him in a uniform. He was one of those easy, loose-jointed men with a nice sense of timing in his hands, but an absent, casual air about his legs. They followed him around, rather than going ahead of him. He sat there, one foot flat on the floor, the other rolled over on its side with the white label of the composition sole staring at me. I could see he had spent some time picking at it. When a farm boy gets around to pants and shoes, and stops finding nice, loose scabs on his knees, he turns to the label, the gum, or the tar on the soles of his shoes. Five years in the army had not put an end to that. Now any man who could grasp the importance of that would be quite an asset, a Creative Native—but more to the point he might write a book a few natives might read. There's no doubt in my mind the importance is there. There in the room, in the straight-backed chairs, the flowered paper, the lone wolf under the winter sky, the three wild horses, the oak-veneered table with the doily from Yellowstone National Park, and in the picture of the old man, on his last birthday, with Viola's five red-headed kids. Stokes, every one of them. It was part of the old man and the old woman, part of the young man and the young woman, the hot afternoon dullness, and for the moment it was part of me. No doubt about it. That accounted for the silly way I felt. That accounted for the fact that Clara Muncy, née Cropper, staring through the curtains at the field of grain, was carrying on about where it was she thought I was born. A white house with an American flag. She remembered the flag, as when they drove up she had to climb down from the buggy in order to make sure, in her own mind, that was the place. It was. She had brought a basket of Ivy's diapers for me to wear.

What was the point of all this? A connection of some kind. My Aunt Clara is not a talkative person, she hasn't time for abstractions, and she could see, with her own eye, that I was there. But the connection. That was the important thing. It had to be established. I had to be born again. There's nothing unusual about that story—except the feeling I had, sitting there, that I had never understood it before. The connection, that is. The important thing. Not the mother, nor the child, but the basket of soiled diapers.

There's a story in the family, on my mother's side, that my Grandmother Osborn started west with her man, her Bible, and her cane-seated rocking chair. As things got bad she had to give up both her man and the Bible, and to keep from freezing to death she had to burn the chair. But first she unraveled the cane-bottom seat. She wrapped it around her waist, and when she got to where she was going she unwrapped it, put it in a new chair. Her kids grew up with their bottoms on it. That cane seat was the connection with all of the things, for one reason or another, she had to leave behind. Which was what these women were doing with me now. They were putting a cane seat, an approved one, in my bottomless chair. Making the connection. The rest would follow, naturally.

Now the trouble with a feeling like that, a sentiment, or whatever you want to call it, is the way you feel when it slips away from you. I've reached the point where I spoil a good many fine sensations because I know, while I'm having them, that they won't last. In an hour or two, a day at the most, I would wonder what the hell it was, if anything, that I was connected with. I would fall back on my work, my troubles, my wife and my kids. Real things. All of them. The connection would be on that busy party-line that was too much for our mothers, our fathers, and for ten or twelve million of their kids—like me. Small town expatriates, all of us. The smart thing is to say there is no connection, but you can't get over the feeling that your Grandma, or the old man, were very much wiser in the matter than you managed to be. That's the kind of feeling I admire, but after a good deal of experience I find it leaves me unconnected with myself. You have to tinker around the best you can. To make a connection with something, I spread my feet, which are large, and looked at the carpet on the floor. Rural Oriental, a fine Axminster. Under my feet there was a little nap, but where the old man rocked there were strands of burlap, like mop droppings, worn into the floor. Under the rug, however, there was still the floor. That was a connection, of a kind, and I stretched out my legs, as I have to if I want to get into my pants. My pipe was in my pockets somewhere.

"Watch what you're doing," my wife said, "you're wrinkling

her rug." I pulled my feet in again, smoothed it out. The center of the rug was pretty well worn away. For some reason or other, maybe for no reason at all, I bent over as if I was trying to look at it.

"If you're lookin' for the figure—" Clara said, "you're just about ten or twelve years too late."

"That was a mighty nice rug," said the old man, "Ax-minister." He pushed his glasses up and said, "You know, I don't think I ever looked at it. I never saw it, and here it is too late." He turned from the rug to look through the screen, at the glare over the road. His eyes were the soft faded blue of his denim bib. "No, come to think I did look at it," he said. "It was nice."

"I got a load of grain," the old man said, "out there near the barn. Just settin'." He pushed out of his rocker, stood up, and looked at his watch.

"It's set for a week," Clara said, "another day or two won't hurt it."

"Told Roy'd bring it in."

"You have to take it in?" Clara said.

"No, I don't have to," he said. "I could leave it just settin'. I could let it rot."

"You have to wait till folks is here you haven't seen for thirty years, your own people, to run off to town."

"You been to town?" the old man said.

"No—" I said, "we come in from the south."

"I should think you'd want to see the town," he said.

"It's been there a good while," Clara said, "and from the looks of things it'll stay there."

"I remember it pretty well," I said, and I didn't particularly want to see it. Not with the old man. He'd like to walk me into the Feed Store and say— "Any you men remember this little fella?"

"If you're going in," my wife said, "you can take Bobby in for a haircut." She ran her hand through his hair, which wasn't any too long, but the old man's hand had pretty well mussed it up.

"Used to be a man named Cahow," I said. "Eddie Cahow, next to the bank."

"He's not next the bank," said the old man.

"No—"

"Lee Stacy's between him and the bank."

"But he's still there?"

"Was last Saturday morning," the old man said. He held a match to the stove lid and said, "Gettin' sixty-five cents now for a haircut." He felt his head. "Comes down to about a penny a hair."

"Peg-GEEE!" said my wife, and we turned to look at my girl, standing in the corner, with a large desk inkwell over her head. She was looking for the price stamp or the Made in so-and-so label. I don't need to tell you where she picked that up.

"What's got into her?" said the old man. Peggy put the inkwell back on the table and scooped up the cat, letting her bottom sag.

"You like the kitty?" my wife said.

"That ain't a kitty, that's a cat," said the old man. "An' he don't like it. Holdin' him like that makes him sick." Peggy put him down on the floor, wiped her hands. The old man put his hand on her head and said, "Used to clip Viola in the summer. It's cooler. Always clip the dogs."

My wife opened her mouth, so I said— "What about Viola, Clara?"

"She'll be here," Clara said, "time you two get back."

"She bringin' Mother Cropper?" Jenny said.

"It's a proposition," Clara said, "to bring her or to leave her. If you bring her she won't let you buy but one kind of gas."

"Time we brought her," Ivy said, "ran out of gas between here and Clay Center. Nothin' but Sinclair in Clay Center. Wouldn't let me put it in."

"Think it was Ed—" the old man said, "had to drain his tank. Put in two gallon of Sinclair on top of her Texaco."

The story goes that Grandfather Cropper was tight in his breeches, and a railroad man, when boys like myself, *any* boy, that is, were in Sunday School. In the course of time Grandfather Cropper was a Brakeman on the C.B.&Q., and a Fireman on the Atchison, Topeka and Santa Fe. He was killed in the Rockies, near some pass or other, when his boiler blew up. As I remember,

he died a hero's death. All through school I was apt to confuse Grandfather Cropper with all the Greek heroes, who died, as I seemed to gather, in some kind of pass. I suppose an epic is how you feel about something. The first epic of my life was the last run of Grandfather Cropper, Fireman first class, between Trinidad and Raton. Strangely enough, Grandma hardly said anything. She just happened to say it often, at the right time and place, with a good many looks out the window, as if she had been there. She always began with just what it was she had put in his lunch pail, that evening, and the fact that the apple he preferred was a Macintosh. I gathered that he wouldn't touch an apple not a Macintosh. That's a small thing, in its way, but it's the stuff heroes are made of, and Grandma Cropper knew a hero when she saw one. She had had, on the other hand, no forebodings at all. I felt this was largely because Aunt Clara had been full of forebodings, and Grandma would have nothing to do with such things. Bats in the belfry, as she called them. She sent him off without a foreboding, chicken sandwiches in his lunch pail, a Macintosh apple, and a clean pair of Fireman's overalls. During the night, though, she did wake up and think of him. As it turned out, that was twenty minutes after the boiler blew off the cab, so it was not, whatever else it was, a *fore*-boding. As for what it was, that was her own business. When she was asked to go and recognize him—with her fare paid, and three meals in the diner—she knew it was not till that moment that he died. He lived for twenty minutes, that is, which was a good fifteen minutes longer than the Engineer, and the dog they had in the cab. There wasn't too much to recognize, but anyone that knew him as well as she did, with the mole on his thigh, knew it was Milton Cropper and nobody else. Grandmother wasn't one to stress anything, but she stamped her right foot, her hand pushing the knee, whenever she spiked that talk of Clara's about forebodings. She also stamped it when she told a funny story—to make sure I got the point—and as I was usually stretched on the floor I could see her foot. It was small, and she was vain about her feet. Her high shoes were laced tight every day, though it killed her during the summer when it got hot, and her feet tended to swell. As an epic is how you feel about something, it was no mystery

to me when all the Croppers, the boys, that is, took to rail-roading. They were men, and they wanted to lead the hero's life. I wanted to lead it myself, but the last time I saw Grandma, as I say, was thirty years ago.

"What's Kermit doing now?" I said.

"He's on the Streamliner—" said Clara. "He's on the run between Omaha and North Platte."

"Ohhh is that an engine—" said the old man, "shooos along there about a hunderd miles an hour—" he watched it roar by, "but I think he liked that old mountain engine best." He tipped back his head, blinked his eyes, "—had one with nine big wheels on a side, and two of them big pistons, just a-pushin' an' a-pullin'. Said it would pull anything. Said if he threw a rope round one of them mountains he'd pull it away." My boy came around in front to look up at him. "Yes sireee—" said the old man, "nine of them big wheels, higher than a man, and two of them big pistons, a-pushin' an' a-pullin'. A purty sight." He raised his right hand over his head. "Nine of them big drivers on each side, half a block long with no more than the tender, but just nothin' for a stack," he put up his thumb, "just a pimple," he said. We looked at him. "So she'd look streamlined, take the wind." The boy swallowed, and the old man went on, "Well, says I, why don't you hitch her up to Madison county an' tow us over there, say around Colfax, where it rains a little more? Well, says he, if I knew where it was it rains like it should, that's what I'd do. An' bygolly he would. Off we'd go a-pushin' an' a-pullin', the smoke a-pourin' out of the stack, an' the whistle flat—" he wiped the whistle flat with his hand, "at hunderd mile an hour you can hear it, hardly see it at all."

I've never been able to explain to my wife what it is I dislike about electric engines, since they were so clean, so powerful, and made so little noise. I looked at her. She was impressed all right, but not favorably.

"Is the whistle for the crossing?" the boy said.

"What it used to be for," the old man said, "but at a hunderd mile an hour says he's sometimes there before the whistle is." He took his hat from the dipper handle, put it on his head.

"Bobby—" my wife said, "would you like to have your hair cut?

Would you like to ride to town and have your hair cut?"

"No," said the boy.

"Well, that's where you're goin'," the old man said. He took the boy by the hand, and just as nice as you please they walked out in the yard. "We're goin' to get our hairs cut," he said, "anyone comin' along?"

"You go along and show him how," my wife said, then she turned to reach for Peggy, missed her, and watched her run toward the barn. She kept at it, quite a little run for her, till she had the old man's other hand. "What's got into her?" she said, then looking at me, "Don't stand there and gape, do something!"

As a matter of fact I was sitting gaping—but I stood up. I gave the dipper a tap as I walked by. I stopped at the screen, whistling a bit, then I walked out in the yard and pulled the seed-head from a long stem of grass. With a little trouble I got the white tip between my teeth. The tassel bobbing, I mosied out in the direction of the barn.

When I got to the garage the old man had the doors propped open, and I could see the bicycle tires on his Model T. There was a new coat of paint on the California top.

"Is that the same one?" I said.

"Think I'd buy another one?" He was up front somewhere, pounding on something. He stopped pounding and said, "Don't like to put in more'n a gallon as she leaks a bit, rustin' through on the sides. But she don't seem to leak along the bottom. Just as nice an' dry as you please."

"You get in and out with a gallon?" I said.

"Sometimes I do, sometimes I don't." I heard him unscrew the cap to the gas tank, lean on the hood. "Don't smell any too gassy," he said.

"Suppose we go in my car?" I said.

"I got to haul in that grain—" he came out of the garage to point at the wagon. The wheels had settled an inch or two into the yard. He picked up a small kerosene can, from a wire hook on the box elder, swished it around several times, put his nose to the hole. "That smell gassy to you?" He handed me the can. "There's two these cans," he said, "one's gas, one's coal oil, but with my nose like it is I can't tell which is which."

"This isn't coal oil," I said.

"Gas then—" he said, and went off with it. I heard him pouring it, slowly, into the tank. "Take it all in all," he said, "finest car he ever built. Not so much ahead, but like a mountain engine when she's in reverse." He put the can in the back seat and said, "I take them blocks from under the wheels?"

"Yes—" I said. I heard him squeeze into the seat, slam the door. "You got the kids up there?" I said.

"We're goin' to get our hairs cut," he said, then I heard the magneto, buzzing like a fly trapped in a mason jar. A blue cloud of smoke shot out of the exhaust, the body throbbed with a kind of palsy, she bucked twice, then suddenly jerked out of the garage. She swung around in a half moon, grazing the bark on the box elder, rattling the harrow, then pulling up, suddenly, facing me. The old man held the wheel like he had a live snake in his hands.

"Dang!" he said, cool enough, "I always forget about that spark."

He kept his hands on the wheel, and lowered the spark with his crooked finger. The palsy stopped, but a soft, lolling roll began. "Well, you comin'?" he said. As the kids were in the front seat, beside him, I had to crawl over the door in the rear. He had a winter top on the Ford, which is a fine thing when it's freezing, but a little less than hell in the summertime. I held on to the braces, and we puttered down the drive.

"Don't she run sweet?" the old man cooed.

"Mighty nice," I said, and carefully shifted my weight, to the inside, when we made the turn. The old man went on, but I didn't hear him, as that part of the road is washboard, and I had the feeling the Ford was falling apart. The old man's hands, gripping the wheel, were a soft, vibrating blur. We went over the rise just east of the farm, barren now except for a few stumps, but once a fine orchard with apples as big as your head. Clara made pies out of one of them. I thought I'd mention that to the kids, as it had impressed me as a boy, but just as I leaned forward the old man put on the brakes. I lost my hold on the braces, spilled over on the kids.

"Dang—!" He said, "I come off without my grain." I looked

at him and he said, "Guess I still get so excited, when I'm drivin',
I can't seem to remember anything." He turned the spark down
and we sat there, brooding, and after a while our yellow dust
came up and went by.

I couldn't go through that again so I said, "Suppose we take
it in tomorrow, Harry? Clara said we had better be back by five
o'clock."

"Tomorrow's Sunday," the old man said.

"What about Monday?"

"Now that's an idea—never thought of that." He makes
these cracks, as I said, with such a dead pan, his faded eyes
blinking, that you don't know whether you're being ribbed or
not.

"I'll have to run in for Peg," I said, "so why don't we wait
and go Monday?"

"You got an awful smart daddy," the old man said. "Yes
sirreee." He looked at the kids and they nodded, swallowing.

I felt pretty relieved, so I said, "Wasn't it around here that
I used to ride? I used to ride that old mare with the green eyes."

"She was blind as a post," the old man said.

"You're tellin' me?"

"Had to tell you then, more than likely have to tell you
now."

"Well, she could find her way home," I said.

"A good thing," he said, and leaned out of the seat to point.
A dead branch, without a strip of bark, hung across the road.
"See that tree?" the old man said. They nodded. "Your daddy
hung up there—seat of his britches—till your Grandpa came
along, with the hayrick, let him down."

"Now that isn't quite true," I said, and leaned forward to
get in a word. "Old Bess left me there, all right, but I climbed
down, walked home by myself."

"Think mine is the prettier story," he said. "What you fellas
think?" They agreed. "Point is—your daddy was hooked by his
britches in the tree."

When you have two kids who were born and raised in an
apartment, on East Fifty-third Street, something like that, about
their daddy, is interesting. I found it interesting myself. I don't

know as I could say, offhand, where I stood in their estimation, but it was easy to see that I had come up a peg.

"I used to ride old Bess every day," I said.

"Myyyy she was gentle," said the old man, "she was as gentle and nice as the day is long." He wheeled over in the gutter, where the road was smoother, and we could talk. "Got an old one right now, just like her," he said, "fine Roman nose, four pretty white feet. Pretty as a picture. Won't do a thing but eat."

"In the barn there was a buggy," Peggy said. "Why didn't we go in the buggy?"

The old man leaned out of the car to spit. He never could spit very well, for some reason, and it came back to streak the isinglass curtain. The curtain on the driver's side was the coffee color of his moustache wings. "Mitch used to say Grace"—he wiped his mouth—"was the prettiest thing he ever seen. Up and down from a buggy, my she was a sight to see." That was my mother. That was the way he referred to her. According to Mitch, for the old man, was according to Hoyle. Mitch was the first of the family, maybe a year or two older than Harry, and the old man seemed to think a good deal of him. "According to Mitch—" he went on, as if he had read my mind, "Grace Osborn was just about the finest woman that ever was." Clara had never said either yes or no to that. She'd heard it a good many times, and I would say the finest thing about my mother were the things that Clara Muncy never said.

"Now I'm goin' to stop here," the old man said, and pulled up at the STOP sign on the main highway, "not because I think I should, but because it's the law." He looked at my kids, one at a time, then we leaped out on the highway, the horn tooting, and headed toward Lone Tree.

When the old man first came to the plains there was a rolling sea of grass, and a lone tree, so the story goes, where they settled the town. They put up a few stores, facing the west and the setting sun like so many tombstones, which is quite a bit what a country store has in mind. You have the high, flat slab at the front, with a few lines of fading inscription, and then the sagging mound of the store, the contents, in the shadow behind.

Later, if the town lasts, they put through some tracks, with a water tank for the whistle stop, and if it rained, now and then, they'd put up the monument. That's the way these elevators, these great plains monoliths, strike me. There's a simple reason for grain elevators, as there is for everything, but the force behind the reason, the reason for the reason, is the land and the sky. There's too much sky out here, for one thing, too much horizontal, too many lines without stops, so that the exclamation, the perpendicular, had to come. Anyone who was born and raised on the plains knows that the high false front on the Feed Store, and the white water tower, are not a question of vanity. It's a problem of being. Of knowing you are there. On a good day, with a slanting sun, a man can walk to the edge of his town and see the light on the next town, ten miles away. In the sea of corn, that flash of light is like a sail. It reminds a man the place is still inhabited. I know what it is Ishmael felt, or Ahab, for that matter —these are the whales of the great sea of grass.

"How's it over your way?" the old man said.

"Clear on the starboard," I said, and he gave her the juice, a good swig of the spark, and we jumped the tracks.

The last time I was in Lone Tree was the 4th of July, twenty-eight years ago, the day that Dempsey thumped the hell out of Carpentier. I was sitting on a stack of *Police Gazettes* in Eddie Cahow's barber shop. My Uncle Harry was flat on his back, with a salt-and-pepper cloth between his chin and his knees, and Eddie Cahow had just finished lathering him. Sprawled out that way, his hands crossed on his stomach, the old man looked a good deal like a corpse, or a man that Eddie Cahow, with his fancy bottles, had raised from the dead. The fight was coming in over the air, or the wireless, as it was called, and the Magnavox speaker was on the shelf right over my head. Everytime Dempsey knocked the Frenchman down, Eddie Cahow would give the old man a nick, then lean back to wipe the bloody lather off the blade. As you probably remember, Dempsey knocked him down a good many times. When the old man sat up in the chair he didn't look much better than Carpentier, as his face was plastered with little strips of toilet paper. I don't think he remarked that at all. He stepped out of the chair, flexed his knees, took out a

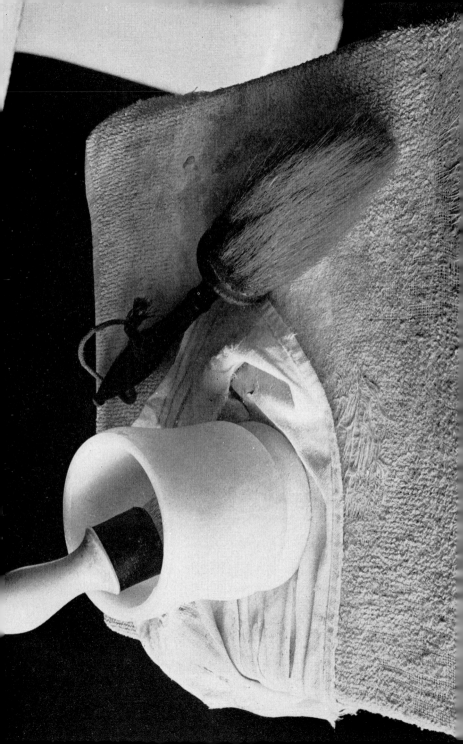

handful of change and ten-penny nails, then stood there sorting out the nails, putting them in his mouth. He gave Eddie Cahow three buffalo nickels, then he turned and offered me an Indian penny with four or five nicks in the edge.

"Seems to me," he said, munching the nails, "anybody knock me down that many times, take more than a little countin' over me to get me up." I took that for what it was, a good piece of advice. We stood there while he put on his tie—it was the 4th of July and he had to wear one—then he took my hand and we walked out in the street.

Now we puttered twice around the block—he didn't want to park where they had the parking meters—then he found a spot, a free one, under a mulberry tree. He raced the motor, shot up the spark, then switched her over to the magneto, letting it buzz while he looked at the kids. "Got a blue-bottle fly in that motor," he said, "little rascal wants out."

"You fellas give me your hands," he said, "an' we'll go down here an' get a cool drink." As the three of them pretty well covered the walk, I lagged behind. There were four or five men standing on the corner, their thumbs hooked in their bib straps, and they began to strop and hone, like a barber, as the old man walked up. "Here's where we get a drink," the old man said, and took my boy by the seat of his pants, tipped him up, and dipped his face in the splash. If there's any one thing that boy hates, that's it. He won't let you put a hand on him, except to button his pants. I thought he would drown in that water, but he never said a word, though his eyes popped and his mouth opened, like a fish. The old man put him down and said, "How was that, wet enough for you?" And the boy nodded his head, soberly. Then he did the same dam thing with the girl. I would have given ten years of my life to have had Peg there, on the corner, staring at the soiled bottom of her precious little girl. His hand pretty well covered her drawers, but for a kid who wouldn't use the word bathroom, or hold up her fingers, it was something she could write home about. He let her down, then had a washy swallow of water himself. He hadn't said a word, or made a sign, to the four or five men standing there, watching him, or acknowledged the fact that I was part of his party, the father of the kids. But as he stood there, filling his pipe from an old sock, which he used for his tobacco, it dawned on me that a good deal was being said. Without anyone opening their trap it was perfectly clear, to everyone present, myself included, that the old man was proud as hell of my kids. Or his kids, put it that way. If they *hadn't* been his kids he would have been the first to speak up about it, but as they were, nobody had to say anything. Everybody was free, and undisturbed, to take this fact and look at it, to drop it on the tongue, like snuff, and get the full flavor while it lasts. The old man filled his pipe, left a sulphur streak on the faded seat of his overalls, then stood there with the match over the bowl, preparing to speak. It was the tribal way of calling for attention, raising your hand.

"How'd you say your New York city water compared with that water there, Clyde," he said.

"No comparison," I said, although I hadn't had a drop of it. "City water is frightful," I said, using that dam word.

"That's what I hear," the old man said, and struck another match. He used this one to light his pipe, then he gazed at the men looking at him.

"You remember Will?" the old man said.

"I think I do—"

"Well, that's his boy—" the old man took his pipe out of his mouth, pointed the stem at me. They all considered me for some time, as my wife considers herself in the mirror, soberly, in spite of the silly hat on her head. "Born—" the old man said, and turned on his heel, looked at the grain elevator to get his bearings, then pointed his pipe over the roofs and trees of the town. "Born right over there, where Boyd lives. Born right in that house."

"See he's got your high forehead," an old wag said, referring to my retreating hair. They all thought that was pretty sharp, but nobody laughed. I got the feeling it would be a serious mistake to laugh. A little vulgar, as a matter of fact, what you might expect from a city slicker, a traveling salesman, with his bag of canned cracks and mechanical jokes.

"When I seen the little fella—" the old one said, "first thing to cross my mind was Ivy. Couldn't tell you why, but that's who it was."

"Was Ivy a towhead?" said the wag.

"He was fair," said the old man, flexing his knees, "with what you call a high forehead." They all shuffled their feet, stropped a bib strap or two, or turned to spit in the dust. I felt like a canary in a private conclave of whooping cranes. "Well—" said the old man, "you fellas ready for a hair cut?" Then he put his hands on their heads. They stood there. "We fellas got our hands full," he said, "we got to go an' get our hairs cut." He let his hands drop, and the kids hooked on to his thumbs. "We got to do a little shoppin'," he said, "suppose you go on down and save us a place?" He stepped off the curb and swung the kids over the street. "Whoops-a-daisy," he said, and walked them across the street, into the shadow of the awning. Over the awning, under a peeling coat of paint, I could see the faint legend EOFF'S GENERAL STORE. A gold and black Atlantic & Pacific sign had taken its place. In the window there were cartons of cornflakes, a poster reading FRESH BABY CHICKS, and a maltese cat, sprawled out on a bin of soap flakes, asleep. I took a mouthful of the water, spit it out, and wiped my mouth with the back of my hand.

I stopped in Howell's drug store to buy a card showing the Platte River bridge, the north end of it, where a boy named PeeWee had once nose-dived in the sand. He didn't break anything, as I remember, but there was gravel in his hair for the rest of the summer.

"Those cards are three for a dime," said the girl, and stopped chewing her gum to spin the card rack. Her head spun with it, silently, like a record about to play. "One is five cents," she said, thinking I'd missed the point. "If you buy three you get one for nothing."

She was young enough, still in her teens, but she had the soft hanging flesh you see on the arms of middle-aged light house-keepers. I always seem to see those arms folded, like a machine in the resting position, waiting for someone to press a lever, or a button, and start it again. Looking at her reminded me not so much why boys leave home, as the fact that they had been leaving it, now, for a good many years. You can't produce a girl like that overnight. It takes breeding to produce a very bad egg, as

well as a good one, and the chickens left behind were getting
inbred, a breed in itself. If you want to skim off the cream every
night you've got to have the whole-milk every morning—Lone
Tree didn't have it, what she had was skimmed milk. Life in the
woods was not what it used to be. The fountains spring up and
the birds sing down, but everybody else took a train for the east,
for New York or Chicago, or took a jalopy to Hollywood. A fine
place, naturally, for the cream of the crop. I know why it is they
leave Lone Tree, as I left it myself, and I'd leave it again, but it
makes you wonder what the hell we're coming to. This girl was
further from the farm, from the old man and the home place,
than the half million kids with the firm flesh, and the high pollen
count, behind the counters and the windows of New York.

"You want that card?" she said.

I dropped a nickel on the counter.

"You tell him they were three for ten?" The voice came
from behind the half-door at the rear, and it swung open on a
man in a candy-striped shirt. He was wearing a high starched
collar and a black satin vest with several pencils, indelible pencils,
over his heart. He began to roll a sleeve.

"I told him three or four times," she said. "About all I did
was tell him."

"You show him the others?"

"You think I'm crazy?"

The man stopped rolling his sleeve, opened a drawer beneath
the counter and held up, half exposed, a picture card. As I
watched, the lady's fat bottom began to roll. He came forward
three steps and said, "I can let you have them five for a dollar."

"Or a quarter a piece," said the girl.

"No thanks," I said. "Not this time."

"What did I tell you?" the girl said, but he was already gone,
the mirror on the door flashing the street light around the store.

I came out with the card in my hand, and without thinking what I was doing I crossed the street, walked around the
barber pole, and opened the screen. As I did, the chirping shears
and the talking stopped. I looked through the door at a towheaded boy, his ears like handles on a tub, seated on the cushioned
board across the chair arms. A small grey man, with a comb

behind his ear, and spectacles the color of flecked isinglass, dropped them down on his nose to peer over the rims at me. He gave the boy three shots of the sweet smelling water, the color of a soft drink called Green River, then he put the bottle down, raked the comb through the boy's short clipped hair. "Now you stand right there," he said, and he turned for a good look at me in the mirror. He tapped the comb on his sleeve, slipped it behind his ear, and said—"You're an Osborn. That's what you are. You're an Osborn."

"No—" I said, "I'm a Muncy."

"That's your name," he said, "but you're an Osborn. You got Will's hair—what's left of it," he said, "but you're Grace Osborn's boy." Although he'd already doused the boy, he gave him another three shots of the water, mussed his hair, then combed it straight again. I could see he was pretty well pleased with himself. As I say, I'm always a good deal cooler when I know the other fellow is a little excited—

"You cutting that boy's hair," I said, "or you sprinkling it so it will grow?" That was good. He slapped the boy's head as if it was the top of a fence post. Then he stepped back, squinting, as if he saw a loose hair. "And if I were you," I said, following up my advantage, "I wouldn't let the old man hear you talking like that." I crossed the room and hung my straw on the hat tree. A dark-haired young fellow, in a white grocer's apron, was sitting on the bench.

"Freddy—" Eddie Cahow said, "you think I got any business takin' money away from a man with as little hair as that?"

"It ain't legal," Freddy said, "but I suppose you got to make a livin'."

"It lays heavy on me, now and then," Eddie Cahow said. He turned the boy around to face the mirror and had another peek at me, to see if I could take it. As it happens, I can take that stuff pretty well.

"People with high foreheads," I said, "can't help being the object of envy. Some people don't have any. Their hair grows right out of their eyes." Was that me talking? It sounded quite a bit like somebody else. I've got a pretty good ear, and offhand I would say that the old man was taking quite a beating.

"It's eyebrows, these people have," I said, "it isn't nice wavy hair."

"When I looked up and saw him," said Eddie Cahow, "I said B-O-Y, Boy! There goes an Osborn. Now I don't know. Sounds quite a bit like somebody else."

"If I were you—" I said, "I wouldn't let the old man hear me say that either." I said ee-ther, though I think I've said eye-ther for the last fifteen years.

"Funny as a crutch," said Eddie Cahow, and unpinned the cloth from the boy's neck. "There you are, Willie," he said. "A genu-wine G-I Joe."

The boy sat there, looking at his knobby new head in the mirror. There was a short brush of hair at the front, like you find on a used doormat, otherwise he looked quite a bit like he'd been scalped.

"It'll grow back, won't it?" the boy said.

"It'll grow in curly," said Eddie Cahow, "if you pull the white hair from a mare's tail."

"That ain't the way I heard it," I said.

"How'd you hear it?"

"You put the white hairs in a can of sand, and the can in a barrel of rain water. Fresh rain water," I said.

"What'll you get?" said the boy.

"Garter snakes," I said.

"That's the truth," said Freddy. "That's the way I heard it." I looked at him, and he nodded his head, soberly. He had a kind of drawl in his voice, with a blurred jews-harp nasal twang about it. I liked him. "How many good live snakes you average?" he said.

"I used to get four or five green striped ones for every long white hair," I said. "But it had to be white. These grayish lookin' hairs gave me pollywogs."

"A good red hair," he said, "will give you some mighty nice fat crawdads. But who wants crawdads?"

"Not me," I said.

The towheaded kid got out of the chair and felt the top of his head, tenderly. He took the piece of wadded gum from behind his ear, sniffed it, put it in his mouth. "Tell your Daddy that's

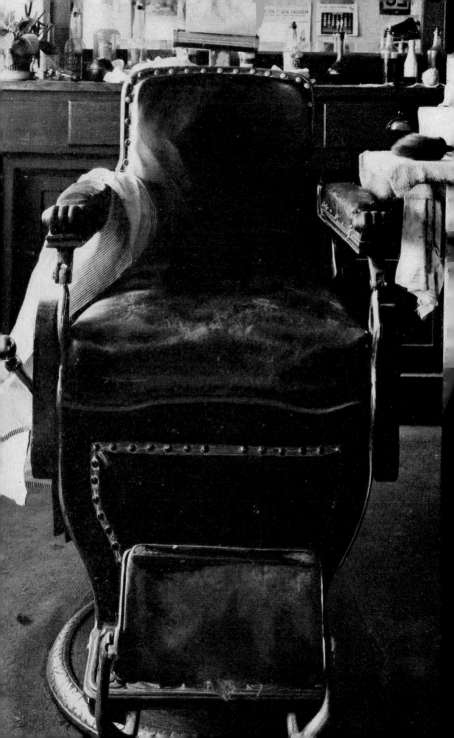

sixty-five cents," said Eddie Cahow. "It's up a nickel. You tell him that." The boy put a penny in the gum machine, got a pink ball. He put it in his mouth and stood facing Freddy and me, his eyes rolling. He had a twitch in his cheek that put quite a wiggle in his right ear.

"You better watch that," said Freddy, "or one of these days you'll just take off. Boy with ears like that is wastin' his time on the ground."

"That's because my hair's short," said the boy.

"It's what?" said Freddy.

"It's gone," said the boy, and picked up his straw, from the pile of magazines, and went out.

Eddie Cahow got a broom from the corner and swept up the boy's yellow hair, left it in a pile with the broom on top of it.

"You in a hurry, Mr. Osborn?" he said.

"I'm just holding a place for the kids," I said. "I've got two kids. The old man will bring them along."

Eddie Cahow sat himself down in his chair and cranked it around so he faced the street.

"I see you only got one chair now?" I said.

"Fool kids—" he said, feeling for the brake, "made a merry-go-round out of it. Tried everything. Only way to stop it was take it out." He looked where the chair had been and said, "How's your daddy?"

"He's dead," I said.

"He marry again?" I nodded. "Was there issue from that union?"

"No—" I said, and Eddie Cahow cranked around for a look at me. "You mind my askin' a personal question?"

"Why, no," I said.

"You comin' back, or you just passin' through?"

I raised my hand and felt the scar, a long crease in my forehead, that I've had, now, for some thirty years. A privy door fell open and cracked me there, one Halloween. As Eddie Cahow was facing me I looked through the screen, spotted with flies, just as a farmer with a new straw stepped inside.

"Howdy," he said, absently, and hung his hat on top of my own. He raised his hand to his face and made a rasping sound in his beard.

"Mr. Applegate," said Eddie Cahow, "man here ahead of you is Mr. Osborn." Mr. Applegate nodded his head, tipped over the cuspidor to spit. Then he straightened up and faced the mirror across the room.

"Mr. Who?" he said.

"Osborn—" said Eddie Cahow. Mr. Applegate crossed the room and sat down in the barber chair. Eddie Cahow tipped him back and spread the peppered cloth on his front, wiped the juice from his chin with the towel he held in his hand. "Says his name is Muncy," Eddie Cahow said, "but his mother was an Osborn. When your mother's an Osborn that's what you are." He wet the towel and packed it around Mr. Applegate's face. "There was five of them girls," he said. "Seems to me it was Will who married the young one. There was Violet, Marian, Mabel, Winona—" Eddie Cahow stopped to work up a lather.

"Grace—" said Mr. Applegate, glowing through the towel. "Think he married Grace."

"Think he did," said Eddie Cahow. "Thought of it myself." He unwrapped the towel and said, "B-O-Y Boy! My she was pretty."

"They was all pretty girls," Mr. Applegate said.

"She sat right over there," said Eddie Cahow, "right where you're sittin'. No. No, she didn't. She sat over there where she could look out—and you could look in." Mr. Applegate raised his head, his face covered with lather, but Eddie Cahow put out his hand, pushed it down. "I suppose you had a look at the farm?" he said.

"No—" I said, "not yet." Then I said, "We no more than just got here. We're staying out with the old man now." Eddie Cahow slowly stropped his blade on the heel of his hand. Facing the mirror, he said—

"It was such a nice place folks used to drive by just to look at it."

"That where they had the hedges," Freddy said, "cut to look like birds and bees?" Mr. Applegate started up again but Eddie Cahow pushed him down. He tipped his head back and slowly shaved his neck.

"John—" he said, "you wouldn't happen to know who's

The Birthday Song
(TYPEMUSIC PRINT)
165
Wonderful Words of Life
166
Dare to Be Brave, Dare to Be True
Dare to Be Brave, Dare to Be True
Tell Me the Stories of Jesus
167
KIMBALL
CHICAGO.

farmin' the place now?" Mr. Applegate rolled his head to the side, pursed his lips, spit through the lather. He rolled it back without saying anything. "Makes a big difference," Eddie Cahow said, "whether you know the people or not. If you know the people you get the feeling they're still on the place." He faced the mirror and said, "What you hear from the girls, Mr. Osborn? Now Winona was a fine girl—what you hear from her?"

"I'm afraid I don't write too often," I said

"But she's well?" I nodded. "She ever get married?"

"As far as I know Winona never got married," I said. I cleared my throat and said, "No, she never got married. Think she took care of Grandpa till four, five years ago."

"She was a fine girl—" said Eddie Cahow, "but a little proud. A little God Almighty. I sometimes wondered if that had something to do with it."

"I think it did. When she got to know better it was too late."

"I just wondered if that was what happened," Eddie Cahow said.

He wet the towel and washed off Mr. Applegate's face. He rubbed some bay rum between his hands and worked carefully on Mr. Applegate's jowls, squeezing out a ribbon of tobacco juice, which he wiped off. "I always wondered," he said, "if Winona got around to getting married. But I can see she wouldn't. She probably passed the right man up right here."

"She all but said as much," I said.

Mr. Applegate raised his head and Eddie Cahow unpinned the cloth. He shook it out on the floor while Mr. Applegate looked at his face, front and side, then wiped the corner of his mouth with the back of his hand. Pushing up, he wiped the back of that hand on the seat of his pants. They were still dark in the seat, but fading light on the calves and thighs, and his watch made a pale full moon in his denim bib. He faced the mirror to put his new straw on, level, with both hands.

"Pride goeth before the fall," said Eddie Cahow. "The old man used to say that. He was quite a preacher."

"He was a God-fearin' man," Mr. Applegate said. We waited for him to go on but he turned and slipped his right hand into his pocket, took out a coin purse, with brass clips, and shook some change into his palm. He put a dime and three nickels into Eddie Cahow's hand. Three two-penny nails he left out and put in the pocket of his shirt. It was ironed flat, and he had to pick at it.

"Thirty-five now, John," Eddie Cahow said, and pointed at the writing on the mirror. "Corn's two dollars a bushel and a good shave is thirty-five."

Mr. Applegate had put away his purse. He blinked his eyes.

"Say you give it to me next time," Eddie Cahow said, and Mr. Applegate walked to the screen and raised his right hand to the man who was waving from the passing caboose. Then he opened the screen, stepped out, and walked away.

"Where's them kids of your'n?" Eddie Cahow said.

I got to my feet and looked through the screen in the direction of the general store. A small crowd of people were standing around the old man. I thought he was just showing off—I could see the taffy colored head of Peggy—before I heard her long, swallowed whimper. The way she cries.

"You go on with Fred, here," I said, and pushed through the screen, tried to keep myself from running. If anything happened to that baby of hers, on a jaunt like this, there would be hell to pay. I hurried up and said, "Uncle Harry, anything I can do?" before I got close enough for a look at the kids. Then the old man turned, and I saw they were both covered with flypaper.

When you've been spraying your screens with DDT, you're apt to forget about the world where they cover the cookies and the cracker barrels with flypaper. More than likely, the kids thought it was something to eat. As I remember, I did, but I'd managed to keep the stuff on the front of my rompers, and out of my hair. Peggy's soft brushed curls were full of it. There may have been an argument of some kind, as she had found it necessary to put her hand, covered with the stickum, smack in the middle of the boy's head. The old man was trying to pull it loose. He was not tickled. When he looked at me his face was flushed.

"These your kids?" he said. I nodded. "When kids as grown up as these never heard of flypaper," he said, "they ain't mine. They ain't Muncys."

"They never saw the stuff before," I said; "how do you expect them to know what it is?"

"All I'm sayin' is," he said, "they're your kids. They ain't mine." He folded his arms on his chest, forgetting about the dam flypaper. His hands were stuck beneath his arms. "Now what am I going to do?" he said.

"All I know is," I said, "they're your hands, they're not mine." At that everybody laughed but the old man himself. He stood there, blinking. I got Peggy's hand out of the boy's hair, and my own pretty well covered, then I held the kids apart, one on each side of me.

"You got 'em apart," the old man said, "by stickin' you all together." He spit in the dust. "Now what you goin' to do?"

What I usually do, at times like this, is turn things over to my wife. I looked at the kids, with their matted hair, then I looked down the street where Eddie Cahow, standing at the screen, was waving at me. If it hadn't been for that, the old man would have had me stumped. I left him there and crossed the street, dragging the kids, as I was in a hurry, and Eddie Cahow held the screen open for us. I dragged them in and said, "Mr. Cahow, if I remember correctly, you're the man who can do something about this."

"Like 'em shaved—or the clippers?" he said. The idea of Peggy with a shaved head—the idea of her mother, that is—made me lose my nerve. I just stood there. "Think it'll be clippers," Eddie Cahow said. "Seems I remember your head was pretty knobby." He began to whistle as he took them out of the drawer.

Well, they both stood there, nice as you please, while he ran the mower over their heads, bawling their hearts out, but too sticky and unhappy to move. Fred Purdy stood by and gave us a hand, brushing off the hair as Eddie Cahow clipped it, and in no more time than it takes to shave a peach, the kids were peeled. "Osborn heads, both of them," Eddie Cahow said, and gazed at them, like at a crystal ball. He closed his eyes and felt the knobs behind the boy's ears.

"I see you're still holdin' hands," the old man said, his nose pressed to the screen, and his arms still folded on his chest.

"Now ain't that a purty sight to see a boy and his daddy holdin' hands." I glowered at him, and he swallowed his chew rather than laugh.

"If you think you can manage it," I said, dipping all of our hands into a basin of water, "you might go into the drugstore and get us something."

"You like a strawberry cone?" he said. I turned my back to him. "I'd sure like to be a help," he said, "but right now I got my hands full."

I got my hands separated from the kids, and began to rub them with a wet towel. "Now you leave your hands in that water," I said, and went outside, passed the old man, who was having a confab with another old fool, about the same age. In the drugstore I asked for some cleaning fluid, then I had to ask him to charge it, as I didn't want to risk putting my hands in my pants.

"Doin' a little shoppin'?" the old man said, when I came out. He had pulled one hand free so he could use it to wipe his mouth. As I've said, he can't seem to spit without splashing himself. He followed me back to the shop where he stood at the screen, humphing, while I worked on my fingers with the cleaning fluid. I was so preoccupied I more or less forgot the kids. When I stepped back and looked at Peggy, her head like an Easter egg with a face painted on it, I had to put my hand on the shampoo stand to steady my legs. The boy was a sight too, with his brown face and scalped bumpy nobbin, but there's nothing in the world like a bald-headed woman or a pretty little girl. I walked to the screen and said, "Do you think you could find me a couple of hats, a couple of straws, or would that be too great a strain on you?"

"I'm an old man," he said, "an' I've all but worked myself to death." He shook his head sadly, then he caught a glimpse of the two kids. Without a word he turned, wiped his hand on his seat, and crossed the street.

You don't feel a blow like that right at the time, there's a wide numb area around it, and you're inclined to think you're a good deal tougher than you are. It's only when you cool down that you see what the damage is. In twelve years I had faced my

wife with a nice selection of problems, but nothing in the way
of her golden-haired baby with a bald head. I was thinking of
this when a tall girl, with a nice rattled way about her, came
around the corner, opened the screen, and backed in. She had a
three or four weeks old baby in her arms. This little fellow was
making a racket like expensive mechanical dolls, or the gadget
they use to make babies cry on the radio. She swooped around a
little, looking for Eddie Cahow, and I could hardly get over the
feeling that I was in the booth of a radio studio. That's the way
the real thing will strike a good many people nowadays. They
won't eat fresh garden peas till they've been frozen or canned

"Eddie's in the back with some kids," Freddy said, and the
girl turned to him, handed him the baby. She held up her arm
to look at the damp sleeve of her dress. She was a belle, in a
disordered way, and rocked on her Sears & Roebucks pumps quite
a bit like Peggy walking around in her mother's shoes. "You feed
him?" Fred said.

"All you do is feed him," she said, and took him away, let
ting him soak her other arm. Fred Purdy let his hands sag, slowly
to rest on his hips. You can judge a man by what he thrills to,
whether it's Humphrey Bogart in a good clean murder, or the
feeling in his hands when he passes his first-born back to his
wife. They're both thrills, sensations, and that's what people
seem to like. Just sticking to the idea of the sensation, which is
all murder has to stick to, the man with the baby, rather than the
blood, on his hands, has the better of it. When a man no longer
makes the distinction, and prefers the quick thrill to the long
one, something pretty serious, pretty fundamental, has happened
to him. It isn't hard to account for—the hard thing is to admit
it. The really hard thing for some men is to admit, in their own
hearts, that a good sentiment is just as valid as a bad one. That's
what it comes down to. They're both just sentiments.

Nearly fifty years ago Cahow's shop was a bank, with a
lobby at the front where he put his barber chairs, and in the
back, behind the grillwork, there was a safety vault. When I was
a boy—if I could sit without wiggling—he'd let me stand in the
vault, in the dark, with the door closed. That seemed to be
where he had gone with my kids. Freddy called, "Oh, Ca-how!"

and I saw the vault door swing open, but the old man came into the room alone.

He grinned at me and said, "Thought they'd like it back there, where it's cooler," then he walked over to make eyes at Purdy's kid. "B-O-Y, Boy!" he said. "Now will you look at that." He peered over his isinglasses, wiggled his eyebrows up and down. "Gitsy-gitsy-gitsy, twee-twee, gitsy-gitsy-gitsy, ughll-ughll, gotsy."

"Doesum likum funny manum?" Fred Purdy said.

"AHH-ahhhhhhhHHHHHHHHHHHHHH!" said Eddie Cahow. "Ah-AHHHHHHHHhhh gitsy-gitsy, gotsy, twee-twee."

The screen door slammed and the old man came in with two straw hats. He held the straws between a paper napkin, and another napkin covered his left hand.

"They're in the back," I said, and pointed toward the rear. The old man stood there. "It's cool back there," I said

"Pretty dark, too—" he said. He didn't seem in any hurry to give them the hats, so I took them, walked through to the back. I opened the vault door and said—

"Yooo-hoooo?"

"Yoo-hoo," said Peggy. I stepped in and felt around over my head for the light. It was red, one of these exit lights with the wire like a trapped glowworm. I could just make out the kids, standing there, holding hands.

"Here's a couple nice hats for you," I said. "Farm hats—for wearing on a farm." They stood there and let me put them on. They were a little large, but both kids had full Muncy ears. "You can wear a nice farm hat like that anywhere," I said.

"Can we wear it inside?" said Peggy.

"You can wear it anywhere," I said. "Inside and outside, you can wear a hat like that to bed." I didn't think it would hurt them to buck them up a bit. "A real farmer wears it all the time," I said, "to keep from getting sunburned, sunstroke, and to keep from losing it." Now I'm not in the habit of talking to the kids like that. We talk to them, as Peg says, as equals, or what she calls little adults, and not a word of any of this baby-talk business. Oddly enough, for some reason, I feel like a bigger sap being adult than I do offering them a fine bill of goods. I

have the feeling a fine bill of goods is what they like. "And if I were you," I said, "inside or outside, I'd keep them on. Tight," I said, which, from me, is pretty straight talk.

"OK," Peggy said, and together we marched into the light.

The old man was standing near the window, holding Fred Purdy's kid. The little fellow had stopped yelling, and there was the feeling, the implication, that the old man had had something to do with it. It was his idea. He gave it to you. He was just as dead pan as ever, if that's what you could call an old fool who was trying to tickle young Purdy's feet with his moustache. Something about it seemed to tickle the kid. The old man raised his head and gazed absently at the mirror, giving me time, all of us time, to appreciate him. His eyes were blurred, and there was a tight, set line to his lips. It struck me that the old fool somehow fancied himself as a kind of Madonna, and that we had gathered, like so many wise men, to worship him. A manger tableau entitled Grandfather and Son. There we all were, the clean-cut local boy, the farmer's beautiful unspoiled daughter, the town-character barber, and the old man with the horny hands of toil. And there I was, knee-deep in the alien corn. The prodigal son with his two bald-headed city-spoiled kids.

Where did I fit in this picture? I didn't, that's the point. I was on the outside—in the control room—looking in. On the one hand I knew that what I saw was unbelievably corny, on the other hand I knew it was one of the finest things I had seen. That ought to tell you quite a bit about me. It told me quite a bit about corn. Corn is the connection between my bottom and the chair. It's the cane seat Grandmother Osborn stretched between the long, long ago, and what she knew to be the never-never land. The figure in the carpet, if there is a carpet, is corn. Corn, I guess, is the grass that grows wherever the land is—as Whitman put it—and sometimes it grows whether the water is there or not. No, it isn't the carpet. It's under the carpet. Corn is the floor.

I'm prodigal enough, but as I'm still unrepentant I took my two bald-headed kids, their straws propped on their ears, and came out on the street. As we looked pretty silly, we went up the alley and got in the Ford. We're not accustomed to being together without some kind of talk going on, usually educational,

but we sat there without saying a word. I guess we had picked up a thing or two to think about. When I was a boy I did my thinking under the front porch, in the soft, hot dust, or on the small hole in Mr. T. B. Horde's three-seater privy. From the small hole I had a pretty good view of the town. I could watch the buggies come and go, and on a clear day I'd follow the trains, with their trail of smoke, across the valley to the west. I'd say the privy is the rural chapel, where a man puts his cares in order, or forgets his cares and turns his mind to other things. A good Sears & Roebuck watch, with a fob, or a pair of Monkey Ward green leather shoes. If the watch section happened to be gone a man could reconsider bone-handled knives, ladies' corsets, or the shadowy teams of horses in their nickel-plated harness, pulling a tassel-fringed gig. Any boy who knew his catalogue—from abdominal belts to zinc—and had a three-seater privy along with it, would find the Arabian Nights, as I found them, pretty dull stuff. What in Arabia could compare with a rubber-tired Irish Mail, a Ranger bike, or *your* initials on the back of a gold-looking, stem-wind watch? Yours—carpet or no carpet—for handshelling thirty bushels of popcorn, or by merely subscribing half the people in the county to the *Saturday Evening Post*. But there were no Sears & Roebuck catalogues on 53rd Street. No privy, with a view of the valley, no unhinged door, no sun on your knees, no slow freights or fast grand-daddy longlegs, no buggies with the whip up, flowering, like a cow's tail, no prowling cats or curious peering leghorns, no a-loneliness, nothing but the damned tiled privacy. Places to worry, that is, but no place to think. Where did they go, then, two or three million kids? I'll tell you where they go—where two of them went—they go and hide in a book, which is very elevated and not to be confused with Monkey Ward. They learn to have other silly thoughts instead of their own. When they sense a thought coming on they run for a window, to get rid of it. They run into the living room, bright-eyed, and say— "You want to hear about the moron in the bathroom?" and you all put your martinis down, prepare yourself. "Why did he tip-toe past the medicine cabinet?" says your brilliant little girl. You wait, and she says, "Give up?" Then you give up, and she pouts her pretty mouth and waits until her

mother has stopped talking. "Because he doesn't want to wake the sleeping pills," she says, and nearly everybody laughs, for it really is so funny, and you wonder what the younger generation is coming to. You do, you know, you really do.

"Is this all one day?" Peggy said.

"It's all one day," I answered, before I had time to think it over, put up my guard. She sighed, like her mother, which meant that she would put up with it. The straw hat was not too good for her ears, and her neck had that raw shaved look, but I had got out of touch with the anxiety I was supposed to feel. I couldn't keep my mind on the problem of her head. Her mother would drop dead, we would bury her, and that would be that. Before she died I would like to tell her—as formal announcements are read on the gallows—that shaving her head had done her darling a good deal of good. There she sat, her pretty little mouth more or less shut. The only reason she ever shut that mouth was to show you her pretty little pout, which everyone thought made her so kissable. Just before we left she came home with the verse—

> I'm a sweet little girl
> And I've got a cute figger
> But stay away boys
> Till I get a little bigger.

That made me nearly sick, but I was ashamed to mention the fact. After all, wasn't that the facts of life? Well, bygod, there are some other facts, one of them being that the old man would have tarred my bottom if I had come home with that. My little soul would have been bruised—which is to say the experience would have meant something—as distinguished from a nice ducky chat on the subject of good taste. All this gives a smart kid is a nice sense for the power of dialectics, a flare for public dogma, and private anarchy.

"Is Grandpa coming?" Bobby said.

"If I was him, I'd wait till it was dark," I said. "I'd be ashamed of two kids who didn't know what flypaper was." They were.

"Does he know what DDT is?" Peggy said.

"He knows it's airsuds," I said, "and he knows enough not to put it in his hair, or get his hands into it. Furthermore—" I said, feeling my oats, "if I was you I'd learn to stop, look, and listen, to keep my mouth shut, and my new farmer's hat tight on my head."

Maybe that's the first time I ever offered them a real piece of advice. It was quite an experience, I could see, for all of us.

The old man stopped on the corner to take another swallow of water, gossip a bit, and pick at the bits of napkin stuck to his hands. Then he mosied along under the trees, got into the car. Maybe he'd forgotten about the kids as he stopped to stare at them and their hats. Then he said, "Well, I guess we got our hairs cut all right, didn't we?" They nodded. He switched on the magneto, kicked at the starter, and we were off. As we rattled on the tracks he said, "Dang, looks like I forgot Clara's flour."

"That depended on the grain," I said. "Didn't it?"

"Your daddy's an awful smart man," he said. "Seems to me he's one of the smartest men we seen." We puttered along and he said, "Thinkin' of smart men makes me think of Verne. You hear from Verne?"

"No—" I said, "how is he?"

"What I'm askin' you," the old man said. Then he went on, "My, he was a rascal." He wagged his head. "That boy was full of devilment."

"I liked him," I said.

"Who said I didn't like him?" He switched the match he was chewing to the other side. "He was just about as nice a rascal as you'd expect to find." He spit out the match. "Never forget him walkin' along, just as nice as you please, in that Ku-Klux business, the band a-wheezin' an' a-tootin' and him marchin' as if it was just for him."

"Ku-Klux—" I said, "was he a Ku-Kluxer?"

"Who said anything about him bein' a Ku-Kluxer? Said he liked to march. Guess he was just beside himself when he heard a band."

"Didn't they have to wear hoods, or something?" I said.

"Sheet over his head like a kid, with two little round holes

for his eyes. Thinks I, it was as nice a Halloween suit as I ever seen."

As a kid I thought a lot of Verne, as he was the first black sheep in the family—came back from the War with a strange way of rolling his eyes. He spent a good deal of time sitting on park benches, smoking cigars, and making neat little piles of gold coins on lunch room counters.

"When you goin' to ask me," the old man said, "how it was we knew it was Verne?"

"I was just getting to it," I said.

"Maybe you remember how dogs was always so attached to him? Don't think he owned a dog, but there was a little dog, black-spotted little bitch, she was, and so attached to him she got so she liked to parade herself. There he was, just a-paradin' along, an' right at his heels was that dam dog. Wasn't a man in town didn't know just whose dog it was."

"What was the dog's name?" Peggy said.

"His name was Moses," said the old man. That was all. "Yes sir," he said. "Moses was that dog's name."

There was another Ford in the yard when we turned in. We made a quick pass over the harrow, trimmed the yard side of the hedge, clipped the tails of two leghorns, and stopped astride a hollow log trough. As the motor died he said, "Just remembered I forgot somethin' else," but without saying what, he backed out of the seat, went off with the kids. Under the big elm near the house, where we had played croquet every Sunday, the women had set up a picnic table, covered the food with cheese cloth. I could see the chill on a glass pitcher of pale lemonade. When I was a kid we picnicked at the fair grounds, just south of Battle Creek, and sometimes as many as fifty Muncys would be there. Clara always made the pies. As she had to make them a week in advance there was always a green mould on them by Sunday, and it was my job to dampen a rag, wipe it off. Nobody else seemed to mind, but I think it was there that I got a preference for cake over pie. Mother Cropper's cake had been baked the night before. I was thinking of that when I walked up and stood alongside the table, waving my hand at the army of flies. I didn't see

the old lady at all. I could hear the women in the kitchen, and I more or less took it for granted they were all there, fussing around, and that I was alone. Mother Cropper, as Clara called her, was in the plush satin platform rocker, with a *Capper's Weekly* spread over her head, to keep off the flies. The spotted cat in her lap was asleep. She had one hand on the cat, and the first thing I thought of was some kind of lizard, or snapping turtle, half concealed by a rock. On the table beside her was her shoe box, with a small pack of letters, tied with a string, a reading lens, a glass egg for darning, and a bag of horehound drops. Also several postcards, all of them featuring some picture of cats. She was asleep when I first saw her, but when I turned from the shoe box her blurred eyes were open, blinking, and she had picked up her cane. "She can't see," Clara had said, "so don't expect her to recognize you."

"Now who are you?" she said. "You Verne?" and rapped the point of her cane on the ground.

"No, I'm Clyde, Mother Cropper," I said.

"You think you can josh me?"

"No, Grandma."

"Well, you're Verne," she said, "and you think I'm old and feeble."

"I should say not—" I said.

"Well, I am—but we don't need to think so."

"Maybe you're getting on, Grandma—" I said, but she wasn't listening to me. She pushed off the *Capper's Weekly* and peered dimly around the yard. "Where they got me now?" she said, then she seemed to get her bearings. "Humphhhh—" she said, "just as I thought."

Grandmother Cropper once had the notion that the world and her own kids were slipping, but that *their* kids were a little more what she had in mind. I could see that notion hadn't changed. I sat down on a chair, but she made it clear, without saying anything, that if I was talking to her I could pull up close. I drew up to where her cane was bumping my knees. She sat munching her teeth, something she did even while she was talking, and it gave a castanet flare to everything she said.

"How have you been, Grandma?" I said.

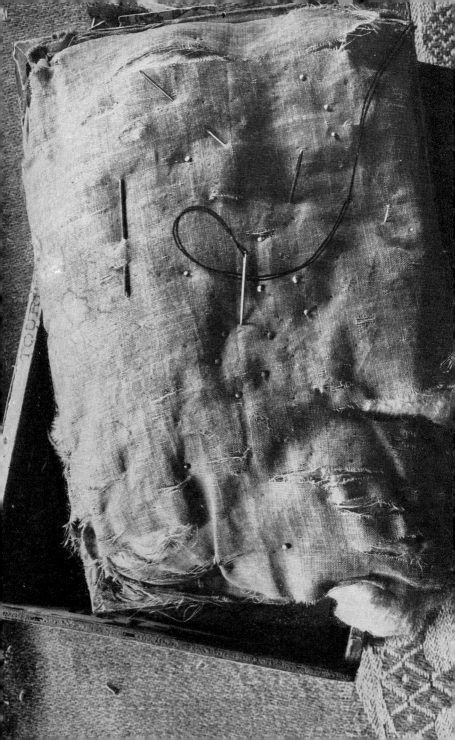

"Sometimes I think I'll go crazy," she said, without hesitation, and peered at me through a cloud of cataracts. She clicked her teeth, and in a sing-song voice—"There's no fool like an old fool, and now it turns out I'm the mother of all of 'em." That struck her as funny, she tipped forward, her head twisted to the right, raised her left leg, and pushed it down, carefully. Her eyelids fluttered, and she made a slight noise through her nose. "I suppose you're married?" she said.

"Quite a while now, Grandma," I said. "Her name is Peggy, we've been married twelve years." I had the feeling none of this registered. "I've got two nice kids," I said. That did.

"Where they at?" she said, and craned her neck around, looked at the yard.

"They're off somewhere with Harry," I said, and when I said Harry her teeth clamped down, she stopped listening. After some time she said—

"You like a horehound?"

"Sure, Grandma," I said.

She pushed off the cat and put the shoe box in her lap. First she had one herself, rattling it between her plates for the sugar, then she passed the bag to me. "When'd I see you last?" she said.

"Twenty-eight, twenty-nine years ago," I said.

"Is that a good while ago?"

"I was about eight years old," I said.

She began to rock, then she stopped and said, "There was three brothers, came from England. Settled in Johnstown, P-A. That was my Grandfather, a Quaker. Said he talked the Quaker language altogether. Came from Wales, settled in Jamestown, in a wooden boat. When they die, they roll them into the sea. He read the Bible, I guess, five or six times. Father used to say, now girls go to bed. Lie there. Tell stories."

"I remember the stories," I said.

"I don't," she said, and put the lid on the shoe box. "But there was a man in one."

The horehound rattled between her plates and she rocked, humming softly. "That's Jesus Saves," she said, "a hymn." She stopped rocking and said, "Grandfather went up the hill, a house with three rooms and a dead cat in it. They lived there. Her and her brother played out on the hill. Said such words. Another said, 'Where'd you hear that?' Men said it to the horses going up the hill." She opened the box, took out another horehound, but held it for a moment in her hand. Then she slipped it in her mouth, slyly, as if she was wiping her lips. "If I don't talk I'm liable to forget it all," she said.

"I know—" I said.

"You know no such thing," she said, and sucked the horehound. "From there to Bowling Green—Montgomery County. Eighty acres, I think. Three men came to get straw. She ran off. When they went away Grandfather said which one you like the best? The great tall one. Said he's married. Then the little one, she said. So she married him." She crooked her head to the side, raised her left leg, pushed it down carefully. There was no sound till she leaned back, wiped the sugar from her lips. "Did I say she married him?"

"Yes," I said.

"Well, she didn't. Till he shot the dog. Indians would have killed him but he went away and stayed three years. Colfax County. She got typhoid and her hair went out and came in. White. He came back and married her."

When I looked at her, her head drooped. I thought she was asleep. Over the paper covering her head I could see the old man crossing the yard, leading a plow horse with my two kids on his back. The horse had a good nose and four white feet, but his rear was so stiff he seemed to wobble. I could hear his hooves chump in the soft, pitted yard.

"Now I'm going to tell you," she said, and raised her hand. "I don't know how many girls it was. Couples. Had to cross the Stillwater, after dark, get in again. Dave Addington said, 'I'm going to kiss all the girls.' Had my hair shingled, but he didn't get to kiss me. Then we went home. To Dr. Hunkle's. He asked to come and I said yes. From then on we went together, seven years, married the day before Christmas," she opened her eyes and said, "eighteen seventy-four."

"How old were you, Grandma?" I said, but I never learned as the screen door slammed and Viola was coming toward me with a pan of hot bread. She stopped in front of Grandma,

opened her hand, and gave her a piece of raw dough."

"Sugar cookies," she said. "Grandma likes it raw."

I remembered Viola as a husky girl with dark eyes, long black hair, and a rather silent way of standing off and looking at you. She had been a little slow, for me and Ivy, and I think she spent a good deal of her time trying to figure out what we were up to. That was still the same. She stepped back, as if she held a camera, to focus on me. Viola is what I would call a handsome woman, a little heavy, perhaps, but solid, and with this penetrating way of listening to you. She had married some boy in the Cropper tradition, a mail clerk on the Missouri-Pacific, but her own feet were still planted on the farm. "She's got six acres of garden," Clara had said, "and four hundred laying hens." She didn't feel it necessary to add that she had five grown kids.

"You was such a little tyke," Viola said, "it's hard for me to place you." That made it clear what all the talk in the kitchen had been. All of the Cropper males were pretty big boys. If I had given too much thought to that I would never have shown up on the farm, as their idea of a man is not very complicated. "Anyhow, you've grown some," she added, which I could see gave her a good deal of relief. She had probably been worried as to how to deal with a little man.

"How is Roy?" I said.

"Now you would have to come right when Roy's at his mother's, with the kids. He gets passes," she said, "so he takes them to his folks in his two weeks off."

"Did Clara tell you," I said, "we plan to be around for a little while?"

"Why, no—"

I was afraid of that. Viola is a Muncy, rather than a Cropper, with the old man's heavy hands and spread-legged stance, but she has an independence that Clara has never trifled with.

"We're going to put up in Ed's place," I said, "as soon as we know how Ed is doing."

"I thought Ivy was doing that?"

"Ivy's been good enough to let us have it first," I said. I could see that she didn't care for that. She liked me well enough, but she didn't think much of that.

"I suppose you know it's a farm?" she said, and turned to

look at the road. "Why it's a hundred twenty acres."

"We've gone over all of that," I said, "and Ivy said he might farm it for us."

"If he can farm for the Bowersox," said the old lady, "he can farm for Verne here, his own kin." She pushed out her teeth, glowered at Viola, then crooked a finger to the cookie dough stuck to her lower plate.

"Ivy's sixty miles away," Viola said. "He'd spend half a day a-comin' an' a-goin'."

"All I know is," I said, "Ivy and Jenny said we could move in." If we're going to be frank, why then let's be frank about it. After all, I'm an obstinate Muncy myself. "I've got a wife and two kids," I said, "and no place to put them. It might be you people don't know what that can be like."

"I'm just thinkin' of the farm," said Viola. "I'm not thinkin' of you or of the house."

"Well—" I said, "I'm not thinking of the farm. I'm thinking of my kids." I looked across the yard, between the barn and the cob shed, where the old mare stood. The old man was letting the kids slide off her rear. He stood there, waiting to catch them, and the sight of Peggie's drawers suddenly made me think of her dolls, in particular a pair of dolly pants. I had picked up a pair for a handkerchief and whipped them out later, at a cocktail party, to wipe some mayonnaise off my tie. "I'm thinking of the kids," I repeated, and wondered how it was, in a matter like this, I had hardly given them a thought. That was Peg's business. What had I been thinking of?

"Well, you want to call everybody?" said Viola, and stepped forward to raise the cheese cloth. The flies hung over the table like the back of a horse. As I turned away the old lady said—

"Now lookee here, see you give him the liver!" She leaned forward on her cane, her teeth snapping, to see that it was done.

"You been to the peas?" the old lady said, and Clara leaned over to pass them to me. I had been to the peas. I had been to the chicken, several times, to the peas in a sauce, the potatoes in a sauce, onions in a sauce, to the coffee, and the butter-yellow ice cream. It left a waxy coating of fat on the roof of my mouth.

In answer to my question Ivy said, "Guess I was in Paris

four, five weeks. It was cold. Don't think I liked it much."

In answer to that my daughter said, "Paris is where the fashions come from," which took care of Ivy, and more or less settled the talk. Five or ten minutes later the old man stood up, filled his pipe.

"You're welcome to try a bowl of this," he said, and offered me his sock, with the hole in the toe. When I declined he belched softly, went into the house. He was back with a new, crisp straw on his head. That was the third hat for the day, but it took me a moment to realize where I had seen that particular straw before. On my two kids. He had bought himself one at the same time. He stood there, lighting his pipe, until we had all made the connection, then he mosied off, his overalls whining, toward the barn. The kids put their saucers down on the buggy seat, followed him. They ran on past him, into the stable, but the old man stopped for his fork, one of two forks, leaning on the wall of the pump house.

"Suppose you run a little water—" Clara said, "so they can wash their hands. Their hands is sticky." He heard that all right, but he didn't stop at the pump. We could hear the soft whine of his walk, and as he stepped into the barn we could hear the hum of the flies over the food. Near the middle of the ice cream Grandma Cropper had fallen asleep. To keep off the flies—her face was sticky—Viola had covered her with a piece of cheese cloth. There was a slight tremor, as there is in a fly net on the rump of a horse.

In answer to what she had been thinking, Clara said, "It's all I can do, when I get him to town, to get him home before it's dark." That reminded her of something. "You forget my flour?" she said.

"We're going in Monday again," I said. "We forgot the grain."

"If it wasn't fastened to his shoulders," she said, "he'd forget his own head."

A statement of fact. There was no malice in it. I tried to remember what there had been, if anything, thirty years ago, but I had neither heard, nor felt, malice when she complained. For sixty years he had put his dirty hats on her clean stove. There

was a place for his hats—she hung them there if she got around to it—but she had never raised her voice, nor thrown them on the floor. "I suppose there's no other place to put your hats but the stove?" she would say.

"There's the dipper—" he'd say, "but I see it's not on the pail." Then he'd take off his hat, stroke the brim, and put it on her stove.

We watched him leave the barn with a light fork of manure. He dropped it in the corral, raking the fork over the top board of the gate, then he paused to fool with a piece of straw on one of the prongs. After some time he got it off, went back in the barn. We heard him slap the sides of the mare, talking to her, edging her over, then he was back, fork in hand, at the door. He stuck the fork in the yard, let himself down on the sill.

"Well, that's that," Clara said, and on her way to the house she picked up a rag, a bandana, that he had dropped.

"While Jenny and me take care of these dishes, why don't you folks walk over to Ed's place?" Clara said.

"It's up to Peg," I said, "if she wants to look at it."

"I know it's perfectly all right," Peg said, "but I suppose it wouldn't hurt to walk over."

Clara walked into the house for the key, came out with it. "For the rear door," she said, "I don't think he used the front door since she died."

I took the key and said, "Now Clara, we'll be back in time to dry those dishes." Then I followed Peg down the walk to the drive, and down the hedge toward the road. The mailbox had once been on a post, near the road, but as someone had knocked it down the old man had put the mailbox, post and all, in an empty milk can. The name H. MUNCY was painted on the side of the can.

"We'll have to write oftener," my wife said.

"Sure," I said, before I realized *that* was an odd thing for her to say. "It's hard to know what to say," I said, but as the trail to the house was narrow and tangled with weeds, I had to go ahead and make a path. There were two scrubby firs in the yard, about thirty feet tall, and placed in front of the house as if they were potted plants. There had once been vines climbing the trellis, but at some time or other they had fallen off, and now grew in a tangled mat near the porch. I followed the trail around to the side, where the late afternoon sun was warm on the tool house, the chicken shed, and the brick-red barns.

"Did you like Ed?" my wife said.

"You know, I hardly remember him," I said. "About all I remember was the Edison Gramophone." As I opened the porch screen she said—

"You sure there's nobody in here?"

"Of course," I said, then I cleared my throat and said, "What in the world do you mean?" She stood there, snapping her knuckles, which irritates me. "I don't know what's got into you," I said, and put the key in the lock, turned it, then let the door swing open into the room.

There was a strong, stale smell, flavored with cobs. As my wife lives a good deal through her nose, I crossed the room to raise the window, but it was pegged down, with some heavy nails at the top.

"These folks get so much fresh air," I said, "they don't like it inside of their houses." I waited for her to pick that up, but she let it pass. Any other time she would have stood out in the yard till the windows were open, and then come in with a handkerchief over her face. Now she came to the center of the room, like you do in a haunted house. My own feeling is that only vacant houses are occupied, or haunted, which is a better word. "This is the kitchen," I said, to say something, and she nodded her head, soberly, as if I had told her what she couldn't see for herself.

"Yes—" she said, and nodded her head up and down. It occurred to me that, right at that moment, we had some kind of understanding that we had learned, over the years, to do without. We were serious. Without being funny, that is.

"Do we burn cobs in that?" she said.

"Cobs or wood," I said, "but I think you'll find a nice bunch of cobs make the better fire." Any other time she would have made some crack about that. I lifted the lid on the range, and she came forward to look at the kindling, with strips of corn husks, prepared for a fire. "That's the way you start a fire," I

said, and looked on the floor for the kerosene can. It was in the corner behind the coal oil stove. "In the winter—" I said, "you can sprinkle the cobs with a little kerosene, if what you want is a quick roaring fire."

"I suppose you do—too," she said.

"You bet you do," I said. I put the lid back on the stove and wondered what it was, since morning, that had come over my wife. "This is a nice little kitchen," I said, "warm and sunny, room enough to eat. I think you'll find you'll spend quite a bit of your time out here." I didn't mean that the way it sounded, I meant that she would prefer the kitchen, like I did as a kid, and more or less live out there. But she didn't pick that up either. She was prepared to, as she had turned to see if I really meant that, or if I was just my old self, pulling her leg. Maybe I wasn't, as she didn't say anything. "Now the thing to remember," I said, "is that Ed's place has inside water. There's an inside bathroom. This place has everything." I left her there to think that over, and walked out of the kitchen into the room where I had played the Gramophone.

What is it that strikes you about a vacant house? I suppose it has something to do with the fact that any house that's been lived in, any room that's been slept in, is not vacant any more. From that point on it's forever occupied. With the people in the house you tend to forget that, the rooms and the chairs seem normal enough, and you're not upset by the idea of a FOR RENT sign. But with the people gone, you know the place is inhabited. There's something in the rooms, in the air, that raising the windows won't let out, and something in the yard that you can't rake out of the grass. The closets are full of clothes you can't air out. There's a pattern on the walls, where the calendar's hung, and the tipped square of a missing picture is a lidded eye on something private, something better not seen. There's a path worn into the carpet, between the bed and the door, the stove and the table, and where the heel drags, the carpet is gone, worn into the floor. The pattern doesn't come with the house, nor the blueprints with the rug. The figure in the carpet is what you have when the people have lived there, died there, and when evicted, refused to leave the house.

"That's Ed's room," I said, and my wife stepped up to look at it. Then she backed away, as if she saw someone in the bed. There are hotel beds that give you the feeling of a negative exposed several thousand times, with the blurred image of every human being that had slept in them. Then there are beds with a single image, over-exposed. There's an etched clarity about them, like a clean daguerreotype, and you know in your heart that was how the man really looked. There's a question in your mind if any other man, any other human being, could lie in that bed and belong in it. One might as well try and wear the old man's clothes. His shoes, for instance, that had become so much a part of his feet they were like those casts of babies' shoes in department stores. Without saying a word, or snapping her knuckles, my wife turned away.

"There's two bedrooms," I said; "we could give this one to the kids." The main bedroom, I seemed to remember, was on the front. I walked up front to look for it, but I stopped at the door, without going in, as the floor was pretty well covered with dead bugs. They had probably been trapped in the house when they took Ed to town. I've been leery of stepping on bugs since I was a boy, in rooming houses, and that dry frying sound still makes me a little sick. On the dresser was a picture of Clara, still looking quite a bit as she does right now, and a picture of Verne some twenty years ago. I was surprised to see that picture of Verne. As I wanted to show it to Peg I started back through the house, for a broom, as I would first have to do something about those bugs.

"Let me get a broom," I said, "before you look the next one over," but I had the feeling, right away, that what I said hadn't registered. She stood with her back to me, looking at the wall.

"Why, that's my Dad," I said. "What's he doing over here?" He was standing with another man and they had a small, dark woman between them. She was wearing a fur-trimmed suit, high laced shoes, and a hat that shadowed her face.

"Would that be Uncle Ed?" she said.

"I don't know," I said, "but that's my mother between them."

I left her there and went out in the kitchen to look for a broom.

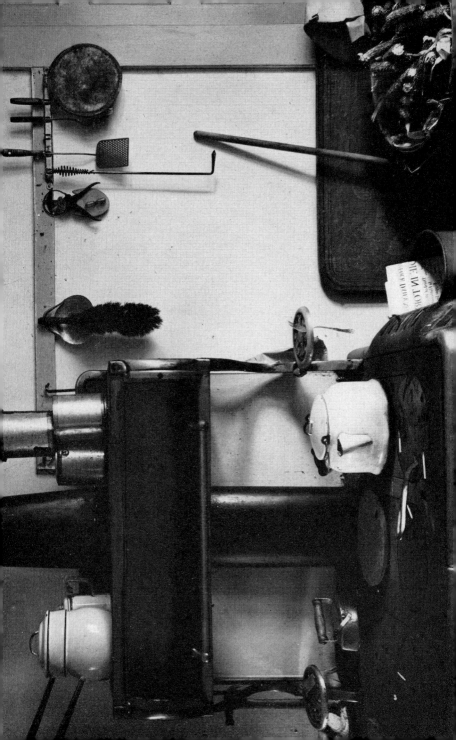

"Who in the world was Walt Mason?" she said.

"Walt Mason?" I said, and came to the kitchen door with the broom. My wife was leaning on the dining-room table, looking at an album of newspaper clippings. "Walt Mason?" I said, then I remembered. "He was a poet." I waited to see what she would say to that. She didn't say anything so I said, "You'll find no pictures in there, if that's what you're hoping."

"No—?" she said; then she began to read—

When I was young I had to go
And till the cornfield with a hoe.
Ah, it was weary work, indeed;
I paralyzed the noxious weed
And scraped the dirt around the corn,
And yearned to hear the dinner horn—

"That will be enough of that!" I said, but she took my word for it. I had to go up and lean over her shoulder, read it myself. "Listen to this—" I said.

The raindrops slug me in the eye
And from my whiskers wash the dye;
They spoil the colors of my shirt
And still they splash and drop and squirt.
One fact keeps running through my brain—
That people used to pray for rain!

"That must have been quite a while ago," my wife said.

"I guess so," I said.

I stood there, and after some time she turned the page. "Listen to this—" I said. I cleared my throat and began—

Backward, turn backward, oh,
Time, in your flight, and give us a
maiden dressed proper and right.
We are so weary of switches and
rats, Billie Burke clusters and peach
basket hats, wads of just hair in a
horrible pile, stacked on their—

"Well, you can read it," I said. I had got that far before I sensed
something was wrong. "What little gem have you found?" I said,
and read another stanza, in my best manner, before Peg turned
from the table and walked away. To make it clear I didn't feel
anything that she might be feeling, I read the fifth stanza very
spiritedly—

I'd be a single man,
Jolly and free,
I'd be a bachelor,
With a latch key.

Now, only a grave man, with a full heart, would have said jolly
instead of happy, joyous, or some such frippery. I stood there,
looking at the page, doing my best to ignore the fact that I felt
more and more like some sly peeping Tom. I put my hand up
to my face, as it occurred to me, suddenly, how people look in
a *Daily News* photograph. A smiling face at the scene of a
bloody accident. A quartet of gay waitresses near the body
slumped over the bar. God only knows why I thought of that,
but I put up my hands, covering my face, as if I was there, on
the spot, and didn't want to be seen. I didn't want to be
violated, that is. The camera eye knows no privacy, the really
private is its business, and in our time business is good. But what,
in God's name, did that have to do with me? At the moment, I
guess, I was that kind of camera.

Was there, then, something holy about these things? If not,
why had I used that word? For holy things, they were ugly

There is rest, there is peace for the frail
    Magdelen
'Tis the Master's sweet voice from Gal-
    ilee's shore.
"I do not con-emn thee. Go sin ye no
    more."

Aye! man, he may sin, and woman may
    weep!
But God is not mocked—"As ye sow ye
    shall reap."
And Heaven at last hears the pitiable
    call,
And the wrath of the Lord on the guilty
    shall fall.

                        J. H. LUCAS.

A PARODY

Backward, turn backward, oh,
Time, in your flight, and give us a
maiden dressed proper and right.
We are so weary of switches and
rats, Billie Burke clusters and peach
basket hats, wads of just hair in a
horrible pile, stacked on their
heads to the height of a mile.
wrong with the maid...
Give us the girls a...
ppear. Give us the...
knew of yore, whose...
me from a hair-dress-...
aidens who dressed...
e view, and just as...
intended them to.
with a figure her...
ioned divinely by na-...
eminine style's get-...
ch year. Oh, give us...
ey used to appear.—
an.) News.

MARRIED MEN.

Who'd be a married man,
  Wretched and sad,
Looking like one who has
  Gone to the bad.

Latchkey forbidden him,
  Never let out,
Unless he will humbly drag
  His wife about.

Slightly imperial
  Conscious of power,
She, like a magpie,
  Talks by the hour.

Who'd be a married man
  Bullied and cowed,
Every day set upon,
  Nagged and rowed?

I'd be a single man,
  Jolly and free,
I'd be a bachelor,
  With a latch key.

These are my sentiments,
  Say what you will,
I am a bachelor,
  I'll be one still.

Please Make Me a Boy.

With the speed of an arrow, through
  time and space,
My memory takes wings, and of
  the place
Where mother and home was the w
  to me,
And nothing else mattered, that I cou
  see,
For there was sweet childhood and
  nocent joy,
Contented to be just a mother's bo
Somehow, the heart feels bleeding a
  sore.
Please make me a Boy for just on
  more.

Take me back again in my moth
  grace,
Let me see the smile on her lov
  face,
As she smoothed the hair away fro
  my eyes
And told me of things high up in
  skies.
How, if I would be true in what
  I did,
The Lord would be with me whe
  was dead.
Unmerciful memory; it hurts to
  core;
Please make me a Boy for just o
  more.

Let me play again by the ba...

If a postage stamp be placed upside down on
the top left hand corner of the envelope it means
that the writer loves you.
If crosswise on the same corner, "My heart
belongs to another and can never belong to you."
Placed in the proper way on the same corner,
"Good-by for the present, dearest."
If at right angle on the left hand top corner,
"I hate you."
The left-hand corner at the bottom, placed the
same way, "I wish or desire your friendship, but
nothing more."
Left hand bottom corner, upside down, "Write
soon."
If put on a line with the surname on the left
hand side it means, "Accept my love."
If upside down in the same position, "I am al-
ready engaged."
If placed upside down in the right hand cor-
ner, "My heart is another's; you must write no
more."
If put crosswise on the right hand corner, it
asks the delicate question, "Do you love me,
dearest?"
If on the right hand side of the surname, proper
way, it says, "I long to see you; write imme-
diately."
At the bottom right hand corner, crosswise,
"No."
At the same place, upside down, "Yes."

P. JOHNSON

enough. I looked at the odds and ends on the bureau, the pin-cushion lid on the cigar box, the faded Legion poppies, assorted pills, patent medicines. There was not a thing of beauty, a man-made loveliness, anywhere. A strange thing, for whatever it was I was feeling, at that moment, was what I expect a thing of beauty to make me feel. To take me out of my *self*, into the selves of other things. I've been in the habit, recently, of saying that if we could feel anything, very long, it would kill us, and that we get on by not even feeling ourselves. To keep that from happening we have this thing called embarrassment. That snaps it off, like an antisepsis, or we rely on our wives, or one of our friends, to take the pressure out of the room with a crack of some kind. That's what I was about to do. For once in my life I didn't, but as I had to do something I went into Ed's room, opened the bureau drawer, and called, "Oh Peg!" When she came in I said— "Ed used to hunt. He used to go off for a day at a time, with a dog and a gun, up the river. When I was a kid there was still a wolf or two around here." I said that, then I closed the drawer, making it clear that we could mind his public business, but leave his private business alone. There were several snapshots on the mirror and I looked at them—for my mother—but I didn't turn them over to read on the back. "Well, she's not there," I said, and came back to the table, pulled out a chair, and looked at an old man's shoes on the seat.

For thirty years I've had a clear idea what the home place lacked, and why the old man pained me, but I've never really known what they had. I know now. But I haven't the word for it. The word beauty is not a Protestant thing. It doesn't describe what there is about an old man's shoes. The Protestant word for that is character. Character is supposed to cover what I feel about a cane-seated chair, and the faded bib, with the ironed-in stitches, of an old man's overalls. Character is the word, but it doesn't cover the ground. It doesn't cover what there is moving about it, that is. I say these things are beautiful, but I do so with the understanding that mighty few people anywhere will follow what I mean. That's too bad. For this character is beautiful. I'm not going to labor the point, but there's something about these man-tired things, something added, that is more than character.

The same word, but a new specific gravity. Perhaps all I'm saying is that character can be a form of passion, and that some things, these things, have that kind of character. That kind of Passion has made them holy things. That kind of holiness, I'd say, is abstinence, frugality, and independence—the home-grown, made-on-the-farm trinity. Not the land of plenty, the old age pension, or the full dinner pail. Independence, not abundance, is the heart of their America.

My wife was looking at me, watching me stare at the old man's shoes.

"What *are* you staring at?" she said.

"The figure in the carpet," I said.

We stood there and she smiled, naturally. That can't be helped: there's a vein of corn in every figure—in a rural carpet—and as she knows there's more than a nap of it on me. That's the mark of any product made on the farm. We stood there, and I watched my girl, Peggy, run along the side of the house, push on the screen, and stumble into the room. When she saw us she stopped, caught her breath, and said—

"We can have it, Mummy—he's dead."

After a moment, solemnly, she took her new straw hat from her new bald head.

"You'd better put it back on," her mother said, and walked over to help her do it. She drew up the slip-knot, tight, beneath her chin. Bobby ran in, his straw pushed back, and stared around the room, a little wildly. He started for the table—"Bob-Bee—" his mother said, "stand right where you are!"

As that didn't sound at all like his mother, he obeyed.

"We're going to move right in," he said. "Grandma said we could move right in."

"We are *not* moving in," his mother said. "The house is too small." I looked at her, and she said, "Run along now and tell your Uncle Ivy, tell him the house is too small for a boy like you." She took him by the hand, firmly, and started for the door. She stopped for Peggy, then called to me, "When you lock the door, don't forget the key."

"No—" I said, and held the screen while she led them out.

I put the chair back under the table, closed the album of clippings, the bedroom doors, lowered the blinds, and came out

on the back porch. I felt like a man whose job it was to close up a church. In this passion, that was the word for a man's house. The citadel, the chapel, of his character. I came out in the yard and looked at the barns, a blue wash of shadow under the eaves, and a string of barn swallows on the power line near the door. Peg was walking the kids across the road. They looked like sunflowers, in their straws, a couple of little fellows that had run away for a day of hi-jinks, and were now being returned to where they belonged. There was no doubt in my mind where that was. All over the plains men now walked to stand at the screen, a damp towel in their hands, look at the sky, and judge what the future held for them. A good idea. It was my sky too. I could hear Clara calling her chickens and I pulled a long stem of grass, slowly, like the old man, and stuck the soft root between my teeth.

As I came in the yard I could hear the whine of the separator. Through the window I watched the old man step away from the bowl, where the crank was whirling, and rest his hands, for a moment, in the small of his back. Clara took away the pail, and left a pan under the spout, for the dripping, and the old man put his hand in the bowl, scooped up some suds. He came out on the porch where the cats mewed at the screen. Rolling up his sleeve, he put his hand through the hole at the bottom, and let the kittens, all five of them, clean it off to the wrist. Mike, the spotted one, was the last to leave. "Thinks I," the old man said, "you think you're just about the smartest little rascal you or any other spotted cat has ever seen." He stood up, dragging his sticky hand the length of his thigh, then he went off, soberly, toward the outbilly.

Someone turned the radio on. The weather. In the room beyond the kitchen I could see Viola, her bare feet on the floor, and between her stocky legs Peggy's patent leather sandals and mosquito-swollen knees. Viola said, "Now there's some things that are right and there's some things that are wrong, and *that's* wrong. Do you hear?"

"Yes, Ma'am."

"All right," Viola said, "just so long as you know." She took Peggy's hand and they walked toward the light, into the living room. The man on the radio stopped talking and saxophones, crooning the theme song, set the stage, briefly, for the cheese food hour. *Stardust*—I heard Ivy's thin whistle, then the music stopped.

"A little bit of that—" Clara said, to no one in particular, "goes a long ways." That was all. She came back to the kitchen, to the quiet, and flushed out the bowl on the separator.

Grandmother Cropper had been showing my wife her afghans. They were spread out on the floor, all around her, and my wife had a few squares, the size of pot holders, lying in her lap. Ivy sat near the window, a sheet of *Capper's Weekly* held to the light. I stood at the screen, facing the yard dark now with tree shadows, and the yellow band of the road, like a streak of cloud, through the shrubs. The old lady munched her teeth and said—

"—after the choir marched in he says, now who is the oldest lady, the oldest mother, here today? Nobody said anything. Then he says, Mrs. Tillie A. Cropper is the oldest lady, the oldest mother, here today." Grandma fluttered her eyelids. "I thought the floor'd sink beneath my feet. I am now going to ask her, he says, to please stand up. I stood up. He walked cross to the pulpit. There was a bouquet of fuchsia. He says, I present this to you today for being the oldest lady, the oldest mother, who is here today. I made a bow, set down. He called on the lady next to me, Mrs. Plomers, but she wouldn't get up." Grandma crooked her head, raised her left leg, then made a light pat on the floor.

Viola came in and said, "Now Grandma—"

"Then he called up the youngest mother," Grandma said. She put out her teeth, like a mask, and stared out from under her Sunday bonnet. Viola turned around, walked out in the kitchen again. "Called up the youngest mother—other end of the aisle— and she rose up. Her child in her arms. He talked nice to her. So when I went out, shook hands, I said— Now who told you I was the oldest lady, the oldest mother, who was here today? Mrs. Cropper, he says, it's a great honor. So I went home. Monday night he came over with Mrs. Plomers, Mrs. Nettie Fields. Now I want you to tell me, I said, who told you I was the oldest lady, the oldest mother, who was there yesterday? Your school teacher, he says. I didn't say anything. She knew."

"You got your box there, Grandma?" Viola said, and came with one of her postcards.

"Then over at Polzen reunion he says, Now who is here in the eighties? Nobody said anything. Who is here in the nineties? Nobody said anything. Well, he says, Mrs. Tillie A. Cropper is the oldest lady, the oldest mother, who is here today. He came over and gave me a vase. Mrs. Furnas said she got it in the ten cent store in Clay Center. I thanked him."

The old man came into the dining room, sat down, took off his shoes, then he carried them with him into the front room, sat down in his chair. He took his glasses from the case on the table, put them in his lap while he rubbed at his eyes. Then he hooked them to his ears, peered around the room.

"Where's the boy?" he said.

"He's asleep—" said my wife. "He was just tuckered out." The old man chuckled.

"Shoulda seen him on Bess. Whoa-giddy-up. Just like he'd been a-ridin' all his life."

"Next reunion I didn't go to—" the old lady said. Her voice was high, and she clamped down on her teeth. "Went to the next one. Saw him over by himself. You're President Polzen reunion, aren't you? I says. I am, he says. I heard you said the oldest lady couldn't get up in the public and talk, I says, but you said the oldest lady there could get up and sing. He laughed and laughed. Then I said, If we're going to sing let us sing *Blest Be the Tie that Binds*. He didn't say anything. When the time came he stood up and said, Let us sing *Blest be the Tie that Binds*. So we did."

"Where's the boy?" the old man said.

"Mrs. Muncy just told you," Viola said, "that he was all tuckered out. That he was asleep. How many times people have to tell you something?"

The old man picked up a paper from the small pile on the desk. He opened it up, belched, and said, "Now there's a level-headed old man."

"Who?" said Ivy.

"Senator Capper," the old man said.

"So I went up to Aunt Min's—" the old lady said, "and here

come a Polzen, nephew of hers— Now who told you, I says, was the oldest lady there that day? Ed Cropper, he said. So there it was, all over town."

Ivy stood up and looked at his watch, left the room. Aunt Clara stalked in, wiping her hands on the dry tail of her apron, and Jenny came in with a straight-backed chair from the porch. She sat on it, slipping her feet out of her tight, mail-order pumps, her toes curling around the side rungs.

"I see here," the old man said, "John Bull's havin' quite a time."

"John who?" said the old lady.

"Says the King never did figure matters out. The Prime Minister says to the King, now I'll write it out and you sign it. The House of Commons says it to the Prime Minister. There's a Parleyment in there. Don't know what they do."

"Don't think they do anything any more," Clara said.

"That Meditrain sea was never much use to anybody, just a cussed nuisance, now she's passed it to Uncle Sam. Here, she says, see you keep them Eye-talians from squabblin'. My, she's smart. So we send over a ship or two—"

"The Prince of Wales would of made the finest one after Alfred," said Clara. "He was always to be found among the miners and the poor."

"All them Royalty is related," said the old man. "Anybody else they put 'em in jail, but if you're Royalty they see to it it's all right. This Queen Victoria turned out most of 'em. The Kaiser, he was a boy of hers, and that there last Cesar of Roosha. No Rooshan a-tall. He was an Englishman."

"From Wales," said the old lady, "—in a wooden boat. When they die they roll them into the sea." Her teeth snapped shut on a piece of blue yarn she had put to her lips, forgotten about. "Harry Muncy," she said, "now where's that picture?" She craned around slowly, like a turtle.

"What picture's that?"

"Now you lookee here," she said, "you know very well there's just one picture." She chewed at the yarn, like a piece of spaghetti, working it slowly into her mouth.

Viola came in and said, "It was there last—" and pointed at

the wall, just left of the bureau. While we looked at the wall she
fished the yarn out of Grandma's mouth.

"When you moved the piano a good deal was upset," Clara
said.

Viola went into the dining room and said, "Well, here it is,
whoever wants it," and came back with a photograph in a small
black frame.

"I want it!" the old lady said, and reached for it. She wiped
the glass on her elbow, then held it close to her face, as if she
would smell it. She counted aloud, slowly, from one to fourteen.

"I keep tellin' you," the old man said, "only twelve of them
is Muncys."

"Lookee here—you think I don't know?"

"Two them girls—" the old man went on, "the nice plump
ones, isn't Muncys. They was Kuhns. Effie and Elsie Kuhn."

"Married Dave and Emerson," Clara said.

"They was Kuhns," the old man said, "but they was Muncys
soon enough. They was together like these Sia-measy twins." He
chuckled. "Them girls was so big all they could do to get four
in the buggy." He gazed off at them. "Come to think, don't
know as they did. Thinks I, more'n a man could do to get a girl
like that down from the buckboard. Think they was great
sitters—"

"They was to the last," Viola said.

"I can see 'em all—" said the old man, "just a-sittin' there."
He looked off, his eyes blinking. "Say on there when that fool
thing was?"

"Eighteen ninety-two," my wife said.

"Bring me that thing!" he said, and my wife got up from the
floor, wiped the glass on her skirt, and handed it to him.

"Lord—it's fadin'!" the old man said.

"You wearin' your glasses?" Clara said, and covered her eye to look at him. He had pushed them back on his head. He let them down on his nose.

"Come to think—" he said, "they never had much as faces. Been thirty years since they had faces." He moved his glasses up and down his nose, focusing. "No, it's worse!" he said.

"Most of us dead and gone, think it would be fadin'!" Clara said. "Same as me an' you are fadin'."

"Now there—" said the old man, pointing, "there is Mitch." He put the splayed nail of his first finger on the tall man, beside the table. "Holdin' the cat," he said. "Told me he was holdin' the cat."

"That's Mitch?" I said.

"Just died—" he turned on the chair and pointed at the wall, between the window and the table. "Died right over there, just south of Sioux City. Eighty-one."

"Eighty one. He was set in his ways—till he took to travelin'."

"A merry-go-round," said Clara. "You call that travelin'?"

"Up and down on a horse," the old man said, "used to make him little sick in the tummy."

"Along toward the last he spun a pinwheel," said Viola. "Think it was Ivy won a kew-pee."

"A wee-gee board," said Mother Cropper. We looked at her and she said, "Told my fortune. Forget what it was."

"Is *she* a Muncy?" my wife said, and pointed at the little one, with no face to speak of.

"Your Aunt May," he said, swinging around like a compass, "over there in the corner. Little west of Falls City."

"She has three the nicest boys—" Viola tipped her head back, looked up at them.

"All the boys had girls, all the girls had boys. Not a Muncy among them," the old man said.

"Them boys is Croppers!" the old lady said.

The old man looked back at the picture. "That Thomas?" he said. He dipped his finger into his mouth, then rubbed a small clear spot on the glass. He peered through it. "No—think it's Emerson."

"Out in Cozad—" he went on, hitching around to face the west. "Last time I saw Emerson he was spry as a kid."

"Had pictures on the wall he hand painted," said Clara.

"One of a dog—" said the old man, "swear he'd come right down and bite you."

"And now he's gone," said Viola, coming in.

"A-men—" the old lady said.

"Think that's Martha," the old man said, "strong as a bull, but, my, she was gentle." He looked around. "Seems like I forgot where they buried her."

"Out in Boone County," Clara said.

The old man wheeled, saw it, nodded.

"Think Maggie May's out there too," he said.

"We never really heard—we don't really know."

"Anyhow, she's gone," said Viola.

"A-men," the old lady said.

"Is Francena there?" Viola said.

"We're all here—" the old man said, "but me an' Roy. We was in Butter County. We was there two, three weeks." He put the picture in his lap, rubbed his eyes. "Indian country, laid as purty as any land I ever seen. Government said hands off. Said this land belonged to people there first. Sioux nation. We drove up in the school yard where the little fellows was marchin' around. Manly little folks. Nice an social as you please. Wouldn't know they was Indians but for them high cheek bones. An' black hair. All have black hair."

"An' now they're gone—" Viola said.

"They was young," the old man said. "Them Indians live forever if a man don't shoot 'em. Heard of an Indian a hunderd an' thirty years old."

"Why that's older than Mother," Clara said, and we looked at Grandma. She was dozing.

"Got to remember she ain't dead yet," the old man said.

"Francena married Clyde Moylan," Clara said.

"Clyde raised some of the nicest punkins, great big fellows, then he took to raisin' pigs. Don't think any of 'em got as big as his punkins did."

"She never liked it in Franklin," Clara said, "but that's where he had his farm. It blows a good deal. The wind is a proposition down there."

"When it stops blowin'," the old man said, "your cheeks puff out." He puffed his cheeks. "Next day it blows 'em right in again."

"An' now he's gone."

"Both of them gone," Clara said. We looked at Grandma but her head was lolling, she was asleep.

"The Muncys live hard an' the Croppers live long," Viola said.

Awake, her teeth snapping, Grandma said, "Harriet Valentine was no Cropper. A Cable. Broke up housekeeping and went to Pickway. There he had his home. Sara Herman was a Cropper. Matthew Lee was a Cable. Now he comes to me an' says you tell me an' I'll take it down. Had pencil an' paper. What was my great-great-grandfather he said, a Cropper or a Cable. I said he was a Cable. He said you don't know. He went away, then at Dayton, Montgomery County, he came in and said now maybe you can tell me if my great-great-grandfather was a Cropper or a Cable. I said Cropper. He said Cable. He had with him the will and your great-great-grandfather willed your great-grandmother the forty acres, the old horse, and three hundred dollars in Confederate money." She stared at us, the paper flowers on her Sunday bonnet softly blurred, then they stopped vibrating, her head lolled, and she was asleep.

"Libby took that paper money an' made a hunderd thousand, if he made a cent."

"An' a lot of good it did him," Viola said.

Clara began to rock. She had been fingering her lips, as if they had been speaking, but she put her hands down and smoothed the lap of her apron. "He'd done better with the horse," she said, "—an' the forty acres."

"All around," the old man said, "we're fertilizin' all around."

"We ain't all—" Viola said.

"We took a lot out, we're puttin' it all back in." He raised his left hand, the cracked palm toward him, the fingers spread. Let's see now, there was Mitch, there was Martha, there was Dave—"

"John and Adeline—" Clara said.

The old man knocked down the last two fingers, raised his other hand. "Then there was Thomas, Francena, Roy, and Maggie May—"

"There was you—" said Viola. He knocked the finger down, then put it back up.

"There *is* me," he said, "I don't count yet."

"And there was Verne," I said.

The old man blinked his eyes. "I can see him just a-paradin' along, the band rootin' an' a-tootin', just for him." He wagged his head. "But you know, I can't see him dead?" He turned slowly on his chair, from one wall to another, shook his head. "No—I can't see him dead."

"He was a maverick," Viola said, "but I reckon he's dead."

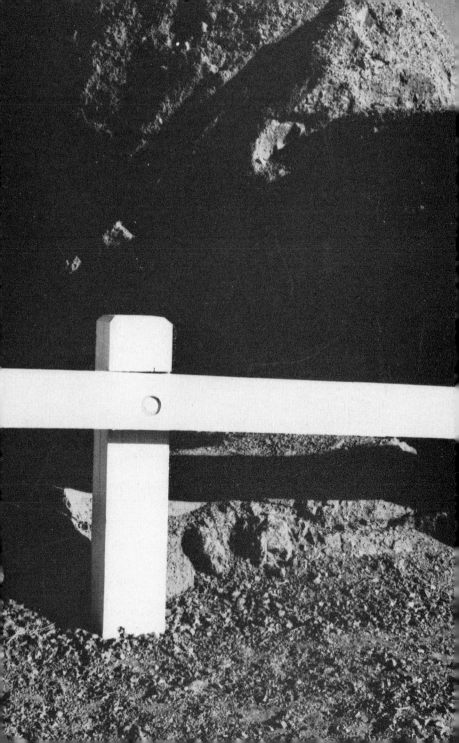

The old man pushed his glasses up, twanged his nose. After a moment he let them drop, and peered at the picture, absently.

"There was Sylvanus and Lorenzo," my wife said.

"My, they was a pair for lookin' alike." He stared at them. "See how Sylvanus is standin' with his hand on Lorenzo's shoulder?" He looked up at us. "That's how they was. They was like *that*." He put up his right hand and tried, for a moment, to cross his fingers. They wouldn't cross. He put the picture in his lap, used his left hand. "They run a store—" he wheeled around, pointed at the window with the blinds drawn. "Harder to get apart than two these sheets of flypaper."

"They was apart," Viola said, "but now they're together again."

"A-men—" the old lady sighed, and tapped her cane. Her head rolled but she fought it off, stared like a stuffed bird. Then, like a sick chicken, the blue lids dropped, settled over her eyes.

"Dang—!" the old man said, "I just noticed how little we're lookin' alike." He dropped the picture in his lap, put his hand down for his shoes.

"I got to get Mother home," said Viola, and began to pick up the scattered afghans. The old man found his shoes, spread the laces, yawned as he slipped in his feet.

"Take that old Bess—" he said, "if I don't go get her she'll stay out all night. Makes her so stiff takes her all day to warm up." He pushed himself out of the chair, slowly. "Guess we're like as two peas." I followed him to the porch where he stopped, centered in the doorway, for a drink of water. He took one swallow, left the dipper rocking on the pail. Turning back to the range he reached for his straw, stared absently at the crown, then put it back on the range—took the nautical number, with the bill.

In the front room, to my wife, Clara said, "Now you folks sure you've made up your mind?"

"When you've got two youngsters," my wife said, "and a man who thinks he's got to have it quiet—"

"Well, you know your own mind," Clara said.

"It's small for us, but it's just right for Jenny," my wife said. "The only thing on our minds is the kids, and if you can just stand them till we find something—"

"Since we're right across the road," Jenny said, "I don't know why it is we can't have Bobby—"

"To hear you talk," Clara said, "one would think you'd never seen your father-in-law. You think for love nor money he'd let anybody have his kids?" She laughed—a little high and false— maybe the first time I had ever heard her. "He's nothing more than an old fool," she said, "when it comes to kids."

I heard the porch screen close, quietly, and I saw the old man take three hasty steps, as through a puddle, before settling down to his stride.

I found him on the buggy seat, under the box elder, using the pruning blade of his pocket knife to scrape the dirt, about thirty years of it, from a croquet ball. As I came up he stooped over, fished around between his legs, and under the seat, then pulled out a mallet, the handle warped to a bow.

"You say that'd warped a bit?" he said. He held it out in front of him, raking the grass. "There was wickets here, somewhere, seems I couldn't cross the yard without trippin' on 'em."

"Seems to me," I said, "any kid worth his salt can make his own wickets."

"That's a hard sayin'," the old man said, and spit in the grass. He pursed his lips, then took them between his thumb and forefinger, gave them a twist, like a cork, then wiped his fingers under his arm.

"He's a smart enough boy," I said, "he's a little small, but I think you'll find—"

"All the Muncys that way," the old man said. "We was all small boys. Then you turn your back—see who it was whistled—and we was all big."

"Peg and me will move on in the morning," I said. "We'll pick up the kids on our way home."

"Where'd that be?" the old man said, and dropped the mallet, pushed himself up.

"Home is where you hang your childhood," I said, as I knew, even as I said it, he had stopped listening. It had been a question he had put to himself, not to me.

"If I don't get goin'," he said, "I'll never get out there, we'll both get stiff. Takes me more'n all day to warm up as it is." He started off. "Boy'll have to come an' fetch us both," he said. That pleased him. He went on— "Well, says I, Sittin' Bull himself must've been the man for that kind of haircut. Well, says, he, an' who is Sittin' Bull?" The old man stopped to ask himself that question, wagged his head. He put his left hand in his pocket, where it came upon a coin. He looked at it. In the house Viola said, "Peggy Muncy, for the last time, you put down that cat. You keep on an' he'll go sick all over you."

"A dime," the old man said. "Where'd I read it was worth four cents?" He looked at the sky, and the hand slipped the dime back into his pants.

Out here you wear out, men and women wear out, the sheds and the houses, the machines wear out, and every ten years you put a new seat in the cane-bottomed chair. Every day it wears out, the nap wears off the top of the Axminster. The carpet wears out, but the life of the carpet, the Figure, wears in. The holy thing, that is, comes naturally. Under the carpet, out here, is the floor. After you have lived your own life, worn it out, you will die your own death and it won't matter. It will be all right. It will be ripe, like the old man.

Nothing happens to a man overnight but sometimes what has been happening for years, every day of his life, happens suddenly. You open a door, or maybe you close it, and the thing is done. It happens. That's the important thing. I watched the old man in his nautical hat cross the yard like one of his harrows, the parts unhinged, the joints creaking under a mat of yellow grass. He stopped near the planter to suck on his pipe, tap the bowl on the seat. On the spring handle of the gear was a white cotton glove, with the fingers spread, thrust up in the air like the gloved hand of a traffic cop. The leather palm was gone, worn away, but the crabbed fingers were spread and the re-inforced stitching, the bib pattern, was still there. The figure on the front of the carpet had worn through to the back.

NOTE ON PHOTOGRAPHS

The photographs of *The Home Place* were taken in Nebraska, during May and June, 1947. As reproduced they represent a compromise between the dimensions of the original print and the novel-size format of the book. Atkinson Dymock's experience and understanding often turned this circumstance to the book's advantage, and his name belongs on the title page as well as here.